Tanner's steps slowed and then stopped on the narrow trail zigzagging up the hill.

He turned to face her. "Look, Miss McGuire, I'm sorry I can't help you. I understand how hard this must be. I'm sorry for your loss, but for your sake, just go home and leave the investigating to the experts."

"I–I can't." A knot rose in Kitty's throat as she struggled to find her footing on the rocky incline. "What you said about me not being around lately for my dad is true. We had...problems, but he was a good man. He doesn't deserve to be remembered for a crime he didn't commit. Besides, this isn't just about me not wanting his memory tarnished. There's more at stake."

Tanner waited, tall and still against a starlit sky.

She bit her lip. How much should she tell this stranger who might hold the key to clearing her father's name?

KELLY ANN RILEY

couldn't wait until she got into the first grade so she could learn to read. The introduction of Dick and Jane in those early readers started a love affair with books that has lasted her entire life. She started penning stories at an early age, and received special recognition for her short stories. Later, she became a reporter and the editor for her high school newspaper.

After earning a B.S. in clinical nutrition and an MBA, she worked for several years as a registered dietitian and director of nutritional services, but she never gave up her first love of writing. Before she was published, she was a finalist and placed in numerous writing contests, including winning Best Inspirational Romance in Romance Writers of America's Golden Heart competition.

Kelly Ann is a member of American Christian Fiction Writers, Romance Writers of America and RWA's Mystery/ Suspense and Inspirational chapters. She now lives in Alabama, where she writes her novels and enjoys many adventures as a youth leader in her church, wife to an engineer and mother to two wonderful children. You can contact her through her Web site at www.KellyAnnRiley.com.

FIRESTORM

KELLY ANN RILEY

Steeple
Hill®

Published by Steeple Hill Books™

STEEPLE HILL BOOKS

Steeple Hill®

Recycling programs for this product may not exist in your area.

ISBN-13: 978-0-373-44403-8

FIRESTORM

www.SteepleHill.com

Printed in U.S.A.

These trials will show that your faith is genuine. It is being tested as fire tests and purifies gold—though your faith is far more precious than mere gold. So when your faith remains strong through many trials, it will bring you much praise and glory and honor on the day when Jesus Christ is revealed to the whole world.

—1 *Peter* 1:7

This book is dedicated to Caroline Dunsheath, a true friend and writing companion, who never stopped believing in me. Thank you, Cee, for your cheerful willingness to read and critique anything of mine no matter how many times you've seen it before. I'm looking forward to many more writing adventures together.

Special thanks to my family, Rick, Ashlyn and Austin, for their love, support and understanding; my mother, Evonne Leiske, who shares my love of reading, and my father, Larry, who inspired me that with hard work I can succeed in whatever I do; Jacqui Wilson, Nancy Latham and all my writing buddies who make this career journey so special; Kelly Mortimer and Tina James for their encouragement and guidance.

ONE

The shattering glass broke the stillness of the moonlit forest, startling sleeping birds into flight and scattering grazing deer in the meadow below. As the last tinkling echo faded away, Kitty McGuire studied the hole she'd created in the back door of the mountain cabin.

Tree branches rustled. A twig snapped. Heart pounding, she whirled and pointed the flashlight beam into the woods. Nothing stirred. Then an owl lifted to the air, its wings silhouetted against the full moon. Kitty sighed as the bird soared toward California's majestic Sierra Mountain range.

The air held a tang of fresh, clean snow from the highest of the Four Sisters' rugged peaks standing like sentries over the little valley. Her father had loved the Sisters, claiming they brought him good luck. Instead, they'd overshadowed his death.

Kitty blinked back hot, angry tears as she punched out the last triangle of stubborn glass and turned the deadbolt. Her hand hesitated on the doorknob as she fought the urge to jump in her Jeep and race back to L.A. She hadn't planned to return to Pine Lake two months after the funeral. Only a murder accusation against her father could've drawn her back to a place overflowing with aching memories.

Tomorrow she'd hunt down the sheriff and the new fire

chief, Luke Tanner, to set the record straight. Her father had died as he'd lived—an honorable public servant—and no one could prove otherwise. Then she could be out of here forever.

With renewed determination, she stepped into the dark kitchen, a blanket of stale air engulfing her. She batted at the filmy web clinging to her forehead.

Spiders.

Kitty shivered and tucked her hair firmly under her baseball cap. Scanning the rafters for any looming creatures, she felt along the wall for the light switch and flipped it. Nothing happened. A fuse must've blown, a common occurrence in the cabin's ancient wiring system.

She yanked open the drawer where her father had kept the spare fuses and stared in dismay at the jumbled pile. She tugged open the next drawer, and then the next. They were all in the same state of chaos. Her fingers sifted through the utensils, matches and other kitchen items. No fuses. Maybe there were extra in the utility box. Slammimg the drawers shut, she turned, and choked back a scream.

A large dog stood in the open doorway, a stream of moonlight gleaming off his fangs. The beast's nails clicked on the vinyl floor as he stalked toward her. A low growl rumbled from its chest.

"Good dog. It—it's okay. Stay!" she said hoarsely. The dog stilled, but the rumbling intensified. Kitty snagged a heavy copper canister of flour. If she threw it and distracted the dog, maybe she could dash outside and close the door.

Sweat trickled down her back. She inched along the counter. Almost there. Lifting the canister, she fumbled behind her for the doorknob, but instead of cold metal, her fingers brushed against something damp and warm.

"Got you!" a husky male voice said. His arm wrapped around her neck, slamming her back against him. The canister flew out of her hand, exploding against the rafters. Flour showered down on them. The dog barked. The man coughed, his chest heaving.

Holding her breath, Kitty wrenched free and darted out the door. She tore around the corner toward her Jeep, but the man tackled her and knocked her into a pile of pine needles.

He pinned her flat. "Freeze!"

She froze. His heart pounded against her spine. Even with her nose pressed into the pine needles, she smelled his male scent of sweat and musk.

"You're not getting away this time," he said.

She twisted frantically under him. Her nails raked his arms. He grabbed her hands and hauled them over her head, knocking off her cap. Hair spilled over her face.

The massive body stiffened. "Hey, you're a woman."

"No kidding."

"You armed?"

"You'd know it if I were." He shifted his weight, and she gasped. "Get off me. I can't breathe."

He rolled to the side with his fingers clamped on her wrist and pulled her onto her knees. She brushed the hair out of her eyes and glared at her captor. Clad in black jogging shorts and tank top, his damp skin gleamed in the moonlight. Dark eyes scrutinized her from a strong-featured face masked with flour.

"Jack, guard." He released her arm as the dog sat, his glowing, canine gaze focused on her. "Don't try anything dumb. The sheriff's on his way. Just be thankful I'm the one who found you and not someone with a shotgun. People are getting mighty fed up with stealing around here."

She sucked in the thin air, trying to catch her breath. "Wh-what are you talking about? *Who* are you?"

He glanced at the cabin and shook his head. "Returning to a crime scene is really stupid, you know?"

Stupid? Her mind seized on a few choice words to call
him, but the sound of crunching gravel from the driveway
heralded the sheriff's car. Kitty stifled a groan. She and Stan
Johnson shared a tumultuous history, and their relationship
wasn't going to improve when he found out why she'd come
back. She watched with growing apprehension as he squeezed
his rotund frame out of the car door.

"Arrest this man, Sheriff. He attacked me," she called
out. Sheriff Johnson strode toward them in heavy boots, his
fingers tapping his gun holster.

"Trouble here, Tanner?"

Kitty's mouth dropped open. Luke Tanner? Of all the lousy
coincidences. No wonder he hadn't identified himself.

"I found her ransacking the kitchen again." Tanner
stretched his long body upward.

"Again? He's crazy." Kitty scrambled to her feet, ignoring
the dog's warning growl. "I just got here tonight and was only
looking for a fuse."

The sheriff's cool gaze flickered over her and Tanner.
"What's that white stuff all over you?"

"Flour," Kitty replied with a lift of her chin, glad more of
the fine powder covered Tanner than herself.

Johnson's thin gray mustache twitched. "Breaking and
entering is a serious charge, Miss McGuire. You should know
that."

She crossed her arms over her chest, ignoring the implied
reference to her past sins. "Give me a break. Since when is it
a crime to break into your own place?"

The sheriff's jaw tightened as he rubbed his evening
shadow. "Yeah, well, things have changed around here. This
property reverted to the town."

"What?" Kitty's voice rose an octave.

Johnson shrugged. "Something to do with funds your

father borrowed on behalf of the fire department. Didn't Pete let you know?"

"No, Pete didn't let me know!" She hadn't seen or heard from Pete Roth, her father's lawyer, since the funeral when he'd informed her Sam had left everything to her. "Okay, maybe Pete tried to contact me, and I never got the message. I've been really busy. This whole situation is absurd. I'll call him right now."

"Can't. Pete left with the missus on a Caribbean cruise. Won't be back for a month."

"How convenient for the town council," Kitty said, hands on her hips. "No one around here to argue. They just take what they want. Well, they won't get away with this."

The sheriff stared at her without blinking and then slid his attention to Tanner. "I'll run her down to the station. You want to come in and press charges or wait till morning?"

Charges? Her stomach constricted as she glanced at the shiny handcuffs dangling from the sheriff's belt.

Tanner shook his head. "Wait a second, let me get this straight. This is Sam McGuire's daughter, Katherine? The firefighter who lives in Los Angeles?"

"Oh, don't tell me you didn't know." Kitty pointed her finger at Tanner. "And nobody except my mother ever called me Katherine. It's Kitty. Got it?"

A muscle in Tanner's cheek tightened as she continued, "I don't know what scam the town council is trying to pull, but the cabin is *mine*. I have a key. Something's wrong with the lock, which is why I broke the back window. The lights wouldn't come on, so I searched the drawers for a fuse."

Both men stood, silent. Kitty gritted her teeth to keep from saying more that might get her into further trouble.

"Miss McGuire," Tanner said. "I can assure you, I didn't know your identity. The cabin's been vacant since the funeral.

I understand before that, you hadn't visited for years, which brings up the question—why are you here?"

Johnson's eyes widened. "Yeah, why now?"

"You know why...." From their blank expressions, they didn't have a clue. How strange. She looked from one man to the other. What was going on here? "Someone called me last night and said you two had turned up evidence that my father set the Wildcat Ravine Fire, which is totally ridicul—"

"Whoa." Tanner held up his hand. "*Who* called you?"

She scowled at his rudeness. "He didn't say—and before you ask, no, I didn't recognize the voice."

The sheriff glanced at Tanner and nodded toward the car. "Wait here," Johnson said to Kitty as they traipsed away. She wanted to scream. They treated her as if she was a pesky mosquito buzzing around their heads, something to shoo away or, if she got too close, squash. Were they nuts? They'd accused her father of murder. Of course she'd be here. Of course she'd be involved.

She took an experimental step toward the house. The dog, which she could now identify as a black-and-tan German shepherd, rose, the rumble back in his chest.

"Okay, okay, settle down." Kitty leaned against a tree, frustration vibrating through her. What a waste of time. She only had six vacation days left from the Los Angeles Fire Department and couldn't afford unpaid leave after inheriting some of Dad's bills.

The two men conferred for what seemed a year, and then the car's engine roared to life. Her mouth dropped open as the sheriff drove away. Who would've guessed? She wasn't going to jail after all.

Tanner reappeared from the shadows. "I apologize for the misunderstanding, Miss McGuire." He snapped his fingers. The growling ceased, and the dog sprang to Luke's side.

"A *misunderstanding?*" Kitty sputtered, following them

around the corner of the house. "That's the understatement of the year. Tell me something, Tanner, where in your job description does it say a fire chief is supposed to be out patrolling for burglars, or in this case, jumping defenseless females?"

Tanner paused at the fuse box, then the kitchen flooded with light. "I'm a neighbor. I was out for a run, minding my own business, until you decided to wake the whole forest by smashing a window. File a complaint against me if you wish, but the fact is, you still broke into town property." His gaze sifted over her, making her skin prickle. "And I wouldn't call you defenseless either. You managed to get your claws into me, but I guess I can't blame you for defending yourself."

He flipped on the porch light and brushed back his black hair, sending up a puff of white before he entered the cabin. "Be careful," he warned. Glass popped under his shoes. "Jack, stay."

She stepped cautiously around the dog that had halted in the doorway. The narrow, outdated kitchen looked even worse in the dingy light. Flour coated the countertops and floor like a fine snow. "What'd you mean when you talked about me returning to the scene of the crime? What happened?"

Tanner brushed his hand along the counter, and flour cascaded to the floor like a waterfall. "Someone broke in here yesterday. Third burglary in town this week. Jimmied the back door open, but at least there wasn't any major damage. Just a few drawers tossed around. I live up the hill, so the town council hired me to oversee this place. I put in deadbolts this afternoon. You may want to check to see if anything's missing."

Kitty nodded as the hairs on her arms stood up at the thought of a stranger pawing through her father's things.

"I filed a report. You would've been contacted soon." Tanner's military-straight posture exuded self-confidence, even streaked with flour. Kitty's insides relaxed some. Maybe he wasn't as incompetent as she first thought. Maybe she could reason with him.

He glanced around the kitchen. "Broom?"

"There used to be one in here." She opened the closet door and handed it to him. He swept the flour into piles as Kitty scooped up glass fragments with the dustpan.

"Why didn't the sheriff take me in?" she asked. "Johnson loved to make my life miserable when I was a kid."

"Since the property is in legal limbo and no real harm occurred, we'll forget about the incident if you do. I'll get the window fixed tomorrow, and you can retrieve any personal things you want to take before I lock up. I can ship the rest to you later."

Kitty bolted upward, dropping the dustpan. "It's two in the morning. Where am I supposed to sleep? The hotel burned down. Even if I decided to go, I'm not driving seven hours back to L.A. tonight. Besides, I can't leave until this stupid accusation about my father is cleared up, and I get my cabin back from those thieves on the council."

Tanner stopped sweeping and scrutinized her. "I suppose there isn't any harm in you staying here until morning."

"You're not listening," Kitty said with a steely edge to her words. "I'm not leaving Pine Lake until my father is off the suspect list. He's not an arsonist any more than you are."

"I'm sorry, but the evidence suggests differently." The bristles from his broom hit the linoleum with such force, clouds encircled her boots.

"What evidence? I have a right to know!"

A muscle twitched in his jaw. "Miss McGuire, go back to L.A. and let us do our jobs."

"Not when you aren't doing your job right!" Her frustration boiled over. Tanner eyes narrowed as he towered over her. She fought the compulsion to retreat and lifted her chin to glare at him.

Tanner sighed. "Look, I know it's difficult, but this isn't just about your father. Two other people died too. I can't compromise the case."

"I already know some of the details. The two construction workers were trapped in the hotel when the firestorm hit, but my dad was miles away and already...gone." She took several deep breaths, fighting the mental image of her father's battered body lying at the bottom of Wildcat Falls. "He had nothing to do with it."

"Even if he was at the fire's origin *before* the fire started?"

Kitty gasped. "How do know you that? Everyone just assumed he saw the smoke and went to investigate."

Tanner turned his back to her. "I've said too much already. The details will be available when the investigation is concluded."

Kitty bit her lip to keep from screaming. "I can't believe this. He was the fire chief for fifteen years and an honorable man. You of all people should understand what he stood for. He protected this town."

Tanner spun toward her, a raw emotion resembling anger or maybe pain flicked across his features before the professional mask settled again. "Just because someone wears a badge doesn't mean they always uphold the vows that go with it," he said in a low, controlled tone. "If your father was involved, as we suspect, then his being the fire chief for fifteen years doesn't matter."

"I'm going to prove you wrong."

Tanner snorted. "How? Word has it you haven't been in Pine Lake for more than three years, except for the funeral. What's motivating you, Miss McGuire? Remorse? Guilt over neglecting your family?"

Kitty's cheeks flamed. "I don't have to answer to you or the sheriff. My relationship with my father is none of your business."

"You're right. My business is to protect the people in this town. I don't have time for this nonsense." Tanner tossed the broom into the closet and the floor shook as he strode to the door. "I'll nail plywood over the window before I go. There are scraps in the shed."

"I can do it."

"Fine. Just make sure you close and lock the door this time."

"Yes, sir." Kitty rolled her eyes. As if she'd forget after her encounter with Fangs tonight.

"If you have a cell phone, keep it handy in case there's trouble. I'll be back in the morning to fix the window and help you move out." He issued a command to the dog, and they disappeared into the night.

Kitty ran to the door. As much as she despised the idea, she needed his cooperation. "Tanner," she called, racing across the moonlit clearing and into the dark woods behind him.

"Wait. I apologize for making you angry." She gasped, her lungs burning. "And I'm sorry I scratched you, even if it wasn't exactly my fault. Please wait."

His steps slowed and then stopped on the narrow trail zigzagging up the hill. He turned to face her. "Look, Miss McGuire, I'm sorry I can't help you. I understand how hard this must be. I shouldn't have jumped to conclusions about you and your father. I'm sorry for your loss, but for your sake, just go home and leave the investigating to the experts."

"I—I can't." A knot rose in her throat as she struggled to find her footing on the rocky incline. "What you said about me not being around lately for my dad is true. We had … problems, but he was a good man. He doesn't deserve to be remembered for a crime he didn't commit. Besides, this isn't just about me not wanting his memory tarnished. There's more at stake."

Tanner waited, tall and still against a starlit sky.

She bit her lip. How much should she tell this stranger who might hold the key to clearing her father's name? People twisted the truth for their own means all the time. She should be cautious until she got all the facts. But when she opened her mouth, the words gushed out like the thaw cascading over Wildcat Falls.

"My grandmother is in a nursing home and the only family I have left in the world. Nana is fragile and Dad's death threw her into a deep depression. I—I thought I'd lose her too." She swallowed hard. "As the fire chief, he was a hero in her eyes. Her belief that he went up on that mountain trying to save lives and died honorably in the line of duty gave her comfort. Now you're claiming he committed arson. Maybe even murder. The shock will kill Nana if she hears that."

"I'm sorry, but the facts—"

"He didn't set that fire. I know he didn't. I feel it in here." She thumped a fist over her chest as she moved closer to him. "Let me prove it. I've taken classes in arson investigation and might provide some insight, unofficially of course. Plus, I grew up here and know this valley like the back of my hand. And despite what the sheriff may have told you about my absence, I still know more about my dad's habits, his friends and activities than anyone else. I can be very useful to you."

Her heart thudded in her ears as she stared into his eyes, willing him to believe her. His granite expression softened and he sighed, his breath tickling her lips. She became aware of how close they stood. She stepped away and her boot slipped on the trail's sheer edge. Arms flailing, she pitched backward.

"Watch it!" Tanner grabbed her shirt and yanked hard. She

slammed against him, her lungs letting out a whoosh of air. Stunned, she didn't move in his embrace. The world stilled as heat radiated off his skin. Chilled with expended adrenaline, she longed to stay enveloped in his sturdy warmth. For a brief moment, she envisioned what it would be like to have someone's strong arms around her like this, assuring her she wasn't so alone in the world. Uneasiness rolled over her. She didn't want to need anyone. After Jordan left, she'd promised herself never to be so vulnerable again.

"You can let go now," she said, her voice muffled in his shirt, but he didn't loosen his hold until she stood firmly in the middle of the path.

"Watch your step. I'm not really in the mood to fill out medical paperwork tonight."

"I'm fine—thank you. Sorry about that…" She stepped farther away, embarrassment heating her cheeks.

She glanced at Tanner. He watched her with an amused tilt to his mouth. "Come by the station in the morning, and we'll discuss your father's case. There are questions you may be able to answer." He turned and resumed his hike up the hill.

"Thanks, Tanner. You won't regret it." Her voice bounced off the massive boulders on the hill. His tall profile melted into the shadows as she rubbed her arms in the brisk air. Her heart still thudded painfully, but something told her it wasn't just from the altitude. This tiny bubble of attraction to the man could be a problem. She should hate his guts for destroying her father's reputation and memory.

The moonlight shone bright enough she found her way easily down the trail back to the cabin. Heeding Tanner's advice, she found a plywood plank and nailed it over the broken window. She'd never been afraid to be alone in the cabin before, but tonight the shadows and quiet seemed ominous. After checking all the locks, she wandered into the living room and sank onto the sofa, too weary to attempt a shower. A cricket sang within the ancient log walls. Was it welcoming her home or warning her away?

She leaned back and studied her parents' portrait over the fireplace. She'd never understood why her father kept the painting after the divorce. But then, she'd never understood a lot of things about Sam McGuire. Like what he'd been doing at Wildcat Ravine before the fire started.

She blinked rapidly as a fresh wave of grief engulfed her. She wasn't going to cry. Tears didn't do any good. She needed to concentrate on the case so she could leave the harsh memories behind and return to her real life. Not only would she run out of vacation pay, but she'd lined up job interviews for a position in arson investigation. A breakthrough here might help her chances to move up in rank.

A scratching noise drew her attention to the hole in the corner where her dad had designed a makeshift pet door to the crawl space under the cabin.

"Max?"

A soft meow answered, and the pet door flap lifted, revealing yellow eyes. The cat sprang through the opening and scampered to the couch. Kitty buried her face into the purring white fur. "I've missed you."

The cat's rough tongue swiped Kitty's chin. Oh, how she'd wanted to take Max to the city with her after the funeral, but she knew he'd be miserable in a tiny apartment. Max was born a mountain cat and enjoyed roaming the woods. Thankfully, her neighbor Mrs. Oakley lived across the meadow and graciously offered to adopt Max and keep him fed. Apparently, he still liked to visit his old home.

Kitty pulled one of Nana's knitted afghans over her legs. Max circled in her lap and settled into a vibrating tubby lump. Kitty rested her head on the cushion, but sleep evaded her as troubled thoughts swirled in her mind.

Her reaction toward Tanner disturbed her. Unfortunately,

he hadn't fit the profile of the inept dolt she'd imagined on the long drive up here. This man wouldn't be easily swayed. His eyes held an unusual intensity and worldly intelligence that intrigued her but also warned her to be cautious. She couldn't let a physical reaction cloud her judgment. She'd use him just like he'd use her to get the job done. Past experience had taught her well. Rule your life with your brain, not your heart. It was safer that way.

It was a mistake, Luke Tanner told himself for the tenth time as he charged up the steep, rocky hill. No doubt about it, he was slipping. How else could he have let the McGuire woman and her sick grandmother get under his skin so easily?

Three months retired from the Bureau and he'd already lost his objectivity. His research revealed Sam McGuire's mother still lived in a nursing home, but Kitty, despite her innocent-looking blue eyes, could be lying through her pretty, pink lips. Her eighty-four-year-old grandmother might be senile and not even know McGuire had died. He'd been fooled before, and the process nearly cost him everything he loved.

He sprinted for the steps to his porch and leaned over, his hands on his knees. Living at seven thousand feet above sea level had some disadvantages—like less oxygen. If he hadn't spent so much time in the Sacramento office the last couple months wrapping up loose ends, maybe he'd be acclimated by now. Jack panted beside him. Luke rubbed the dog's soft ears. "Come on, let's check on Michael."

The dog raced ahead as Luke deactivated the alarm and climbed the stairs to the attic bedroom. The glow from the night-light illuminated the peaceful expression on Michael's face, so unlike the surly one dominating it most days. Jack sniffed the boy from head to foot, and then lay on the rug, apparently satisfied no harm had come to his young charge.

Luke untangled the quilt from around the lanky ten-year-old

body, gently tucking the ends under. "Thank you, God," he whispered, awe in his voice. Even now, six months after the kidnapping, he found it difficult to believe he had Michael back safe and sound. Well, maybe not sound yet, but in time.

Luke smoothed a wisp of copper-colored hair off the boy's forehead and then stepped toward the intercom that connected to downstairs and his father's bedroom. "Dad? I'm back. Any problems?"

"Heard you come in." His father's gruff voice erupted from the small, black box on the wall. "Not a peep out of the kid."

"Thanks for staying up. I didn't mean to be gone so long." He flexed his stiffening shoulders. What a night.

"No problem. With this contraption, I can hear a mouse tiptoe across a pile of pillows. It's been a quiet evening, just what I needed to finish up this book on the John Muir Trail."

"You thinking of taking a hike?"

James Tanner chuckled. "No, just wishful thinking. You know my old knees wouldn't last five miles. You, though, work too hard and ought to take a vacation. Take my grandson camping like we used to do. Spend more time with him. A group from the church goes once a month in the summer."

"I know. I'll check it out soon." Luke's neck muscles knotted tighter. Finding the time for getting active in the church was another reason to get this case wrapped up fast.

"I'd lend you the book, but I need to return it to the library tomorrow."

Luke smiled. He had a sneaking suspicion his father liked Miss Grant, the town's kind, silver-haired librarian. When he wasn't fulfilling his pastor duties at the community church or spending time with Michael, Dad hung around the library. Luke had mixed feelings about this possible romantic development. Logically, he wished his father happiness, but the thought of anyone taking his mother's place twisted his gut.

First Mom, then Miranda. Too much heartache in the last three years. He didn't know how he could've gone on if he'd lost Michael too.

"Night, Dad." Luke switched off the intercom. He gestured to the German Shepherd.

"Come."

The dog followed him down to the kitchen where Luke scooped out dry dog food. Jack stared at the bowl until Luke remembered to give the command to eat, a safety precaution to prevent poisoning. His father had thought Luke overly cautious by purchasing the specially trained dog for Michael's protection, but having Jack gave Luke more peace of mind. *And Lord, you know I need more peace.*

Still too keyed up for bed, he trudged onto the long deck that hugged the length of the house. The crisp, mountain air soothed his hot skin. He leaned on the redwood railing and gazed down at the quiet town huddled next to the lakeshore. Pine Lake boasted clean air, good schools, small-town values and even an active church congregation.

After the horror of their last year in Chicago, the secluded valley seemed like the perfect place for Luke and Michael to start a new life. Luke hoped that with love and his grandfather's spiritual guidance, Michael's troubled spirit would heal, and the child could learn to trust again.

Jack trotted to the railing and whined. "I know, boy, you feel it too. Things aren't right." Luke moved to where he could see the McGuire cabin. Despite the tranquil setting, something sinister brewed in Pine Lake, and he couldn't shake the feeling Kitty McGuire had bulldozed her way into the middle of the mess surrounding her father. How deeply she was involved, he didn't know. Someone wanted her to come back. But why?

"Jack, go inside," Luke said, releasing the dog to his post. Except during school hours and an occasional night run, Jack stuck close to Michael.

Luke moved indoors and caught a whiff of the McGuire woman's light flowery scent on his arms. Her courage and determined loyalty to her father stirred something inside him. A longing he thought he'd buried with his wife. A longing he didn't dare indulge in. Not now. Maybe never again.

Luke sighed and locked up the house. As usual, his timing stank. Who would've guessed after he'd turned in his badge and moved to Pine Lake, he'd be fighting crime again? When Sheriff Johnson, the only person in Pine Lake other than family who knew Luke was ex-FBI, asked him to temporarily assume the fire chief position to assist in the arson investigation, he couldn't refuse. If the town wasn't safe, then neither was Michael. Protecting his son consumed his whole life now.

He headed to the shower. The steamy water washed the intriguing woman's scent away, but an edgy feeling lingered as he toweled off and crawled between the cool sheets. Exhausted, he tried to sleep, but Kitty's parting words, "You won't regret it," kept echoing through his mind.

Luke groaned, rolled over and punched the pillow flat.

Regret it?

He already did.

TWO

"Land sakes, it's Kitty McGuire," a voice boomed over the din of the Monday breakfast crowd at Sarah's Café. "Come give me a hug, child!"

Kitty stood in the doorway and grinned at Sarah Moore maneuvering through the sea of tables. Despite living in an outdoor sports-oriented town in the rugged California Sierra Mountains, the proprietor of the lakeside restaurant consistently wore fashionable business suits and matching designer pumps.

"It's great to see you." Kitty hugged the petite, middle-aged woman and breathed in the familiar spicy scent of Sarah's perfume mixed with citrus from the oranges she squeezed every morning. "I've missed you so much."

"Well, you wouldn't know it on my end." Sarah propelled Kitty toward the table by the front window overlooking Main Street and the lake. "Not an e-mail or phone call in months." Her smile took the edge off the scolding.

"I'm sorry. I meant to call, but I've been so busy with work and classes. I finally made it into the arson investigation program."

"Great news. Your pa would've been proud."

If only that were true. She couldn't remember the last time Sam McGuire noticed or approved of anything she'd done.

Snagging a coffee pot, Sarah said, "Anyway, never mind my fussing. I know you have your own life. This town isn't exciting enough for most young people, unless you're a wilderness enthusiast or ski bum. So, how long are you visiting?"

"A couple days. I have some details to wrap up concerning Dad's affairs," Kitty answered, not wanting to discuss her father in such close proximity to so many other ears. She hesitated by the wooden chair her father had claimed every morning during his nineteen years in Pine Lake. She could almost see him sitting there in his worn blue uniform, pager by his plate, drinking coffee while debating local issues with Sarah's husband, Daniel.

"Are you all right, dear? You're so pale."

Kitty's throat tightened. "It seems so strange not having him here."

"How thoughtless of me," Sarah said, her hand pressed over her heart. "Would you like to sit somewhere else?"

"No, no, this is good. I want to sit here." Kitty eased in the chair. The sooner she learned to deal with the situation calmly and systematically as a professional investigator, the sooner she'd solve this case and leave this town. Permanently.

Sarah poured steaming, fragrant coffee into two mugs and joined Kitty at the table. The older woman sighed and smoothed back a frosted wisp of hair that had escaped her French braid. "Do you know how sorry I am that I wasn't here for your father's funeral?"

Kitty's eyes stung. "Oh, Sarah, please don't apologize. I got your message and card. You needed to be with your poor sister. Is she any better?"

"Not really, but she's still able to enjoy the Florida sunshine. That's something, anyway. Are you sure you're okay?"

"Just tired. I got in after midnight," Kitty said, almost adding, "and wrestled with the new fire chief," but preferred to try to wipe the disturbing image from her mind.

"Poor dear, you must be exhausted, and you have to stay in that filthy cabin all alone. Daniel's been keeping an eye on the cabin for you, but it must be dusty and full of spiders. Why don't you come stay in my guest room?"

"Thanks, Sarah, but I'm fine in the cabin."

"Then I'll send Daniel over with a mop and dust rags. In fact, I'll go with him to make sure the job's done properly. It's the least we can do for you under the circumstances. Clarence is perfectly capable of running things around here." She nodded toward her part-time cook framed in the kitchen window. "I'll call Daniel at the hardware store."

Kitty grabbed Sarah's hand before she could summon her husband. "Whoa, I appreciate you wanting to help, but I'm not a kid anymore. I can take care of it myself." She grinned at Sarah's dubious expression as her gaze swept over Kitty's faded jeans and blue T-shirt.

"Can you? You're still way too skinny. I'm going to see that you eat a decent meal." Before Kitty could protest, Sarah signaled to Clarence. He trundled across the floor and set a plate and a frosty glass of orange juice in front of her. After nodding a solemn hello, he retreated behind the counter.

Kitty smothered a groan as she eyed the mounds of steaming pancakes, scrambled eggs, and Sarah's famous homemade turkey sausage. "Thank you, but I only stopped in for a quick cup of coffee and toast. I'm on my way to the fire station to pick up Dad's personal things."

"That can certainly wait until after breakfast." She stood. "I'm pretty sure everything got packed up after the new chief took over, but Daniel's on duty this afternoon. He'll be glad to help you."

"Oh, it'll be okay. I don't want to cause anyone extra work." Except for maybe Luke Tanner and the sheriff. Obviously, they needed to start the investigation from scratch. She ran her fingertip around the rim of her coffee mug. Had Tanner sent someone over to fix the broken window yet? "Did you say Daniel has been looking after Dad's place?"

"Of course, I told you he would when I called you after the funeral," Sarah replied in an insulted tone.

"But—"

The sound of breaking dishes crashed through the café.

"Oh, that Clarence, now what's he done?" Sarah said. "He can cook up a storm, but he has such butterfingers. I'd better go see what this will cost me. You eat and I'll be right back." She waited until Kitty picked up her fork before marching to the kitchen.

Kitty stabbed at the buckwheat pancakes and took a reluctant bite. The syrupy cake melted on her tongue and despite the knot still in her throat, it slid down, warm and smooth. She sighed and gazed through the lace-edged windows at the sunlight dancing on the deep blue of Pine Lake. She would've enjoyed the food and scenery more if her mind wasn't whirling with disturbing questions.

If the town council had appointed Tanner in charge of the cabin, why did Sarah say Daniel was still looking after it? Didn't they know the town had repossessed the property? Strange. Sarah hadn't mentioned the break-ins at the cabin, or elsewhere either. The café was the town gossip hub, and few events escaped Sarah's knowledge. Maybe she just didn't want to scare her. Or maybe the council didn't want anyone to know what they were up to.

The bell on the door jingled. Kitty nearly choked as Tanner entered. His gaze flicked around the crowd, then lingered on her before he strolled across the room and claimed a stool at the counter.

She swallowed her mouthful of eggs, annoyed that her heart thumped faster every time she looked at him. At least

Tanner's entrance affected others besides her. Men exchanged glances and women nearly drooled behind his back as he opened a copy of the local newspaper. Without a word, Sarah shoved a coffee mug in front of him.

Kitty tapped her foot impatiently on the wood floor. Did she dare join him? It'd probably just give him another opportunity to tell her to leave town. She didn't want to blow her chance of getting into the fire station. Somewhere in there may be a clue as to why her father visited the ravine that fateful day. Maybe he saw something suspicious and decided to check out the area.

She slumped in her chair, drained after the Tanner-induced rush of adrenaline. It wasn't fair. He certainly appeared fresh and well rested. Her entire body ached, and even though she'd shampooed her hair three times, she still wasn't sure if she'd gotten out all the flour.

His thick, ebony hair didn't show a speck of the chalky stuff that turned to paste when water hit it. Brushed back from his wide forehead, the shaggy, unruly waves tumbled down his neck almost to the broad shoulders that strained against the confines of his white T-shirt. The shirt, tucked neatly into black jeans, couldn't hide the strength in his chest and arms.

Her eyes followed the line of his long legs down to the black boots crossed at the ankles. Nice boots, Kitty thought, tucking her own under the table. Her gaze lifted and collided with Tanner's dark eyes. He flashed a grin and hoisted his mug in mock salute.

Heat curled in her stomach, and her face flushed. He obviously enjoyed her discomfort at being caught gawking at him. He took a gulp of coffee and raised his eyebrows as if daring her to do something about it.

She stood, ready to wipe the teasing smile off his face with a scathing remark, but her elbow bumped something on the wall. She turned and grabbed a swinging frame.

"Way to go, Kitcat."

Kitty jumped at the use of her old nickname. Only one person ever called her that. She looked over her shoulder at compelling blue-gray eyes set in a tanned, boyishly attractive face fringed by silvery-blond hair. "Evan Stone, what on earth are you doing here?"

"Eating breakfast?"

Kitty grinned. "No kidding. I meant what are you doing in Pine Lake? Last I heard, you were on assignment in China."

"Actually, Mongolia, and I left there a year ago." Evan spun Sarah's vacated chair around and straddled the seat with his lanky, khaki-clad legs. "So, what do you think?"

"Of Mongolia?"

"No, silly. The photo."

"This is yours?" She sat and studied the breathtaking shot. Two bald eagles clinging together by their talons, tumbled through the brilliant blue sky above a jagged canyon wall. "What are they doing? Fighting?"

He cleared his throat. "Actually, they're mating."

"Yikes. They don't fall to the ground, do they?"

"Nope. When it gets too risky, they break free of each other. You know, like most relationships." Bitterness edged his tone, causing Kitty to glance up. He still smiled, but the wariness etching the corners of his eyes hadn't existed in his younger, carefree days.

She concentrated on the photograph, critiquing it as Evan had taught her when they were kids and Evan was a budding photojournalist. "It's an awesome shot, well framed, very powerful, but yet a vulnerable feeling comes through." She raised her head. "When did you start photographing birds? All you ever talked about as a kid was how much you wanted to photograph war zones and other hot pockets in the world."

"Got tired of living out of a duffel bag." He shrugged. "Figured I'd try something different." He tapped the glass on the frame. "I won the Piedmont Award with this one. You're going to come by my place and see my portfolio, aren't you? I'd tell you it's spectacular, except you know how modest I am."

Kitty laughed with him as she hung the picture back on the wall. She leaned forward on her elbows. "I'm so glad to see you. I've missed you."

"Ditto, kid. I came through L.A. several times but never had time to hook up. I was traveling on location until after your dad's funeral. Wish I could've been here. Don't know why, but I liked the old grouch. What do you say to dinner tonight? We can catch up."

The eager tone in his voice caught Kitty by surprise. Was Evan Stone flirting with *her?* They'd always been just friends, even if her teen-aged heart had yearned for more. What a disaster that relationship would've been. She'd learned the hard way how it felt to have her feelings shredded without his help.

"I'd like to visit, but I don't know if I'll have time. It all depends on how today goes. I need to get back to L.A."

"What's the rush? Your boyfriend waiting for you?" he asked. "Sarah told me about him…"

"Jordan?" She grimaced. "Look, I really don't want to talk about him. He—"

"Sarah said you're going to tie the knot."

Kitty gaped at him. But then why should she expect the gossip to stop just because she'd moved hundreds of miles away. "That was over a year ago. He's long gone."

"What happened?"

"It's boring. Let's talk about something else."

"You might as well tell me." He leaned forward in the

chair he still straddled and propped his elbows on the chair back, resting his chin on his hands. "I'm a journalist and I can't help myself. I won't stop pestering 'til you spill your guts."

"Eww, isn't it considered bad manners to talk about spilling guts in a restaurant?" She tried to joke, but Evan continued to stare owlishly at her. Tenacious as always.

She sighed. "Fine, if you must know. Irreconcilable differences. He wanted kids right away, a picket fence and a wife who wasn't gone for days pursuing a risky career. He didn't want to wait for me to go back to school, either."

"Sounds like a real loser."

"Told you it was boring. But he wasn't all bad, or wrong, in fact. People need to be around to make a relationship work. Spend time together. *You* should know about that."

"Which is why I stick to my policy of no serious commitments to any woman."

Kitty rolled her eyes. "I can't blame Jordan. Look where I came from. Maybe I'm not cut out for marriage. Maybe it's in my genes. Dad was a workaholic who communicated with me less than my cat, and my mother took off and never looked back. Jordan gave me an ultimatum. Quit the department or quit the relationship. I quit him."

"Sounds like you made the wise decision."

"Somehow, that doesn't make me feel better coming from Mr. Love 'Em And Leave 'Em. I can't believe I'm talking to you about this."

Evan grinned. "I am what I am. And since we're both currently unattached, why don't you accept my invitation to dinner? We can have some fun."

At her hesitation, he crossed his arms over his chest and narrowed his eyes. "Surely you still don't hold the window incident against me."

"What window?" Kitty asked startled, thinking of the

glass she'd broken last night. He glanced at the wide picture window beside them. "Oh! Well, of course I do. It was your fault. You called me a city brat and pulled my pigtails. I only tried to defend myself."

"Yeah, with a big stick."

"The stick flew out of my hands by *accident.* You left me to face Sarah all alone."

"It takes a smart man to know when to retreat."

"Or a coward!"

"Now, *that* hurts. As I recall, I was the one in danger." He laughed and squeezed her hand. "Ah, Kitcat, despite our shaky—or should I say *shattering*—beginning, we had good times, didn't we?"

"Yes, we did." Kitty sighed. Not many thirteen-year-old boys would've paid attention to a skinny, shy eleven-year-old tomboy. Maybe he tolerated her because she was gullible enough to believe the sun rose and set by his adventures, which, unfortunately, landed her in trouble more times than she could count. But no matter the reason for their friendship, she'd cherished every moment. Hanging with Evan had been exciting, and in the process, Kitty learned her way down every back alley and dusty trail in Pine Lake. The knowledge had come in handy numerous times when eluding the sheriff.

"How about this?" Evan asked, glancing at his watch. "Let's shoot for dinner together sometime this week or whenever you're free. Call me when you know what your plans are. Deal?"

What could it hurt? Time had patched her cracked heart and made her wiser. "Deal."

"Great, and while you're sampling my barbecued steak, I want an interview. If you haven't heard, I own the *Pine Lake Tribune.*"

Kitty snorted. "You bought that gossip rag? Why?"

"What can I say? It needed me. *Really* needed me," he said with a playful smirk. "I have issues coming out weekly now instead of monthly. And it's no longer just gossip and recipes. I have serious stories in there, plus, of course, exceptional photographs."

"McGuire. We need to talk." Tanner's tone implied *now*.

Kitty looked up at Tanner's flinty expression and extracted her hand from Evan's as irrational guilt pricked.

"I'll be at the station in five minutes." Tanner nodded a greeting at Evan. "Stone."

Before Evan could reply, Tanner proceeded out the door. After a stunned moment, Kitty stood and slapped some bills on the table. "I'm sorry, but I need to go."

Evan scowled as Tanner passed the window. "He has some nerve. A flatlander who's only been here six or seven months but already thinks he owns the town. He speaks and people jump, including you."

Kitty bristled at his tone. "Hardly. We have an appointment." She grabbed Evan's arm and pulled him outside into the pine-drenched air. "Spill. What do you know about him?"

"You interested?" He smirked and nudged her with his elbow.

"Not in the way you mean," she retorted as Tanner climbed inside his pickup. "It's strictly business."

"Right. Business." He slipped on sunglasses and hid the mischievous glint in his eyes. "Tell you what, I'll offer a trade."

She crossed her arms over her chest. "I already said I'd have dinner with you."

"Not enough." He shook his head. "I'll tell you what I know about Tanner, if you'll give first dibs on news about the Wildcat Ravine Fire. That's why you're here, aren't you? I heard the rumor the sheriff wants to pin the blame on your dad."

Her stomach twisted. So, it was common knowledge. "Tanner does, too."

"I'm not surprised," he said wryly. "Do we have a deal?"

"All right, just don't print anything until the investigation's closed. Johnson would love to throw us in jail just for old time's sake," she said as Tanner's truck rolled around the bend and disappeared. "So what are people saying about the new fire chief?"

"You're so easy," he teased, and she slammed her elbow into his ribs. "Ouch. Okay. You know how in this town everyone knows the scoop on people before they've even been here a full day? Tanner's been here for months, and no one knows much about him. Not even me, whose job is to be nosey. But then, we don't exactly run in the same crowd."

"In other words, he doesn't hang out at Harry's Bar and flirt with girls every night?"

Evan snorted. "You think you know me so well. The girls hit on *me* these days. What I meant is he has a kid and hangs with the PTA and church crowd. His father's the pastor of the community church."

"Oh," Kitty said, suddenly disgruntled at the thought of Tanner having a wife. She hadn't noticed a ring on his finger the night before. "I didn't know he was married."

"He's not. Widowed, I think. He's closed-mouthed about it too, although I can't blame the man. The hens around town are already setting out traps to snare him for their daughters. I'm not sure, but I think there's a story there. Something to do with his son. The kid has behavioral problems. Been in detention so many times, he has his own desk."

"That's all you got?" Kitty asked with exasperation. "I spent a lot of time in detention too. So did you!"

Evan shrugged. "All I know is that the sheriff was pretty determined to have the town council appoint Tanner as fire chief. Not many people were eager for the position after what happened." He shot her a contrite look. "Oh… sorry, I didn't mean to imply your dad didn't do a great job."

"He did the best he could," Kitty said, her face heating. "Thinking he'd resort to arson is ridiculous. What motive would he have?"

"Now see, that's the big question circulating on the grapevine." He waited until a couple passed by and entered the café before continuing, "Some say he was furious with the town council for cutting funds to the fire department, and he wanted to prove a point. Others think he dropped one of those awful cigars he always smoked in the wrong place. Oh, and my favorite rumor is the speculation that firemen are closet pyromaniacs just waiting for their chance to—"

"You've got to be kidding! Dad didn't give a hoot what decisions the council made. If the fire department needed something, he found other ways to raise money if he had to. And he respected the environment too much to just drop his cigar butts. Besides, the last time we spoke, he said he'd given them up. As for pyromaniacs posing as firefighters?" She breathed out a disgusted sigh. "Sounds like a bad B movie."

"Hey, I didn't say *I* believed any of it. You asked. I don't know what evidence they found. The sheriff officially told me to butt out, which means they must have something. That won't stop me from digging, though. I'll see if I can get more background on Tanner, and you keep me informed on what you find out about the fire."

Kitty unlocked the car door and slid onto her seat. "I'll give you a call, okay?"

"Here, take my card. My cell number is on the back." The lines on his bronzed forehead deepened. He glanced over his shoulder at the café and leaned closer. "Listen, Kitcat, I wasn't going to say anything, but you know me, I can't mind my own business. You dad was a decent guy, but sometimes things aren't as black and white as they appear. Like with a great photograph, there are layers to everything, depending on what angle you're looking from."

"What are you saying?" Kitty asked, outraged. "Do *you* think my father is guilty?"

"No, of course not, but someone set that fire and…I'm just telling you be careful, okay?" He pushed her door shut and then tapped on the window until she rolled it down. "And keep your guard up around Tanner. My instinct tells me the man's hiding something."

The heavy metal door slammed behind Kitty as she strode into Pine Lake's fire station. She pushed her sunglasses onto her head and blinked until her eyes adjusted to the dusky interior. The large bay appeared deserted. Her boots echoed on the concrete as she followed the path of light to the back office.

"Hello? Tanner?" She stepped around a pile of wet, dirty fire hoses, brushing her shoulder on the side of the nearest fire engine. The sleeve came away black with soot, and the air hung heavy with the acrid scent of smoke.

She glanced up at the truck beds. Someone had packed the engines with fresh hose, but the filthy place was a disgrace to any well-run department and certainly didn't inspire additional faith in the new fire chief.

"Tanner?" Her voice rang out into the bay. Where was the man? He'd demanded she meet him and then disappeared. She shivered, uneasy being alone in the large, shadowy building, which seemed absurd after spending so much of her youth there.

She reached the office and gasped. The battered gray filing cabinets were open, the drawers empty. She maneuvered around mounds of manila folders and paper. What was going on? If Tanner was trying to hide something, his method worked. Finding anything useful to the investigation would be difficult in this mess.

"Tanner!" she yelled for the third time, but only gurgling from the yellowed coffee machine answered her. She sidled around her father's hefty desk. The painful knot rose in her throat again. This was the last place she'd seen Sam McGuire alive. The last place they'd spoken face to face. And argued.

Files had fallen behind the chair. She squatted and examined the headings. Her father's bold handwriting labeled some. The two desk drawers hung ajar. She tugged open the bottom where her father used to store his small, spiral-bound notebooks containing records of his activities, mileage and, most important, notes on daily events. Empty.

She pulled on the top desk drawer, but the railing caught. She yanked harder and something fell with a clunk to the drawer below. She lifted out a gray rock embedded with sparkling minerals.

Fool's gold. She smiled as she rubbed the gold flakes between her fingers. Her father used to take her up to the waterfall and let her pick out pretty specimens to add to their rock and mineral collection at the cabin. Somehow, this specimen must've gotten wedged in between the drawers.

She stood up and smacked into someone behind her. "Oh, sorry." She spun awkwardly and her boots slid on the discarded files. Steely arms caught her as she stumbled, her cheek landing against a white shirt.

"We really do need to stop meeting like this," Tanner murmured into her hair, his arms tightening around her.

THREE

Kitty shoved Tanner away, her heart pounding. "Do you always sneak up on people, or is it just me you enjoy scaring?"

Tanner's amused expression vanished. "Excuse me, but this is *my* office. If anyone was sneaking, it was you." He glanced at her fist. "Trying to steal something?"

"What?" Kitty's mind whirled. His musky aftershave was playing havoc with her already strung-out nerves, but what befuddled her most was that she'd liked being in Tanner's arms.

"What's in your hand?"

"Oh." She uncurled her fingers. "Fool's gold. And I wasn't stealing it. There's tons of this useless stuff around here. You want it?" She tossed the rock to Tanner. "This probably came from my dad's collection. He had a special liking for pyrite."

He examined the specimen and handed it back. "Keep it."

"Thanks." Kitty shoved pyrite in her back pocket. "Too bad it's not real gold."

"I hear there are still gold mines in the mountains. My father likes to research local history."

"Most of the mines have been abandoned. My great-great-uncle owned a small claim during the gold rush but never made much progress. Dad said the tunnel eventually collapsed." She glanced around the office. "Why is everything on the floor?"

He cocked a hip on the desk, blocking the exit. "I thought maybe you could tell me."

The implication of his words hit her, and she sucked in a deep breath. "I didn't have anything to do with this."

"You still have a key, don't you?"

"I don't know. Maybe." She lifted her palms toward the ceiling. "But anyone in the department could get in here."

"Johnson said you had a temper. Smashed the window at the café."

"I was *eleven*. Give me a break. Besides, whoever opened these cabinets must've used a crowbar. If I had a key, why would I bother?" She shoved a drawer shut with her knee.

"Don't touch anything."

"If the sheriff's going to look for fingerprints, he already has a copy of mine and no, you don't need to know why. For the record, Mr. Fire Chief, I stayed in the cabin all night." Kitty wrapped her arms over her chest. "You seriously don't think I'd vandalize the office."

Tanner's dark eyes studied her, and then he sighed. "It crossed my mind, but no, I don't. What were you looking for?"

"Just my dad's personal items from the desk. I know I should've picked the stuff up after the funeral, but I had to get back to work."

"You should've asked permission first. This is an open criminal investigation. You have no right being in here, especially without my permission."

"You invited me, remember?" She mentally counted to ten. "But you're right. I could've waited until you returned." She forced a bright smile. "Last night you said I could see the evidence you'd found."

"Nice try, but as I recall, I said you could stop by and answer some questions before you headed for home."

Kitty leaned toward him, still smiling. "Read my lips, Tanner. I'm not leaving until you drop the case against my dad. You're stuck with me, so get used to it."

He studied her for a moment, his eyes dark and unreadable. "Was your dad as stubborn as you?"

"More."

"That's hard to believe," Tanner muttered, moving to the valley wall map. "I consulted with Sheriff Johnson this morning, and he agreed you might provide some useful insight. Think you can handle being objective?"

She squared her shoulders. "I'm Sam's daughter, bred and trained to be tough."

He looked unconvinced but proceeded. "Let's get to it then. I have a lot of work today." He tapped the map. "As you know, Wildcat Ravine is where the fire started. Your father's truck was found here in the parking area, singed but luckily not burned. We found kerosene traces in the cargo area."

"So?" Kitty moved closer so she could see. "That's not unusual. My father ran a furnace business. People still use kerosene lamps and heaters in the more remote areas. Sometimes he made deliveries while out doing surveillance."

"We found a canister tossed in the woods."

"Where, exactly?"

"Top of the falls." He pointed to the spot where someone had shoved a pushpin.

"Any fingerprints?"

He shook his head. "Burned off."

"Anyone could've left a canister. It might've been there before the fire. The Bronco is a department vehicle and used by other personnel."

"But not everyone smokes cigars."

Kitty's stomach clenched, remembering what Evan had mentioned about her dad being careless. "Again, it could've been someone else. He was giving up cigars."

"Apparently not soon enough. DNA from the saliva on the butt matches his. The cigar had fallen among the rocks, near where he…."

"Fell." She swallowed hard. "But the cigar could've been dropped there another time. Wildcat Ravine was a favorite place of his, yet another reason he wouldn't have started a fire. If he saw smoke he'd go to investigate."

"No one knew he was up there. There's no record he called the fire in."

"Maybe he didn't have a chance to," Kitty said with a sinking feeling as she remembered Tanner's words from the previous evening. The only logical explanation would be that he was up there *before* the fire started. But…why hadn't he called in the report on his radio?

She shook off the first tentacles of doubt and crossed her arms. "You don't have much of a case. There are no witnesses and the cigar is circumstantial evidence. What aren't you telling me?"

Tanner turned from the map, his gaze meeting hers. "Did your father ever mention belonging to an organization called SOLO?"

"Sounds vaguely familiar. What's it stand for?"

"Save Our Land Organization. Started as conservational group, but some of its extremist wackos decided the political channels were too bogged down and took matters into their own hands."

"Go on," she urged when he grew silent.

"In Colorado last summer, the federal government approved a petition to allow developers to build two new ski resorts in a protected area. When it comes to national forests, the government is allowed to trade acreage across the country as long as the total amount of protected acreage remains the same." There was sharp edge to his voice. "The Colorado project was well under way when a fire swept through and burned everything to the ground. When they started building again, another fire was set. They caught a couple of the perps, but the leaders are still at large."

Kitty perched on the desk's edge and rubbed the goose bumps on her arms. "I remember the fires. Several firefighters died, but I don't recall any talk about SOLO. Where'd you get your information?"

"I have my sources. The FBI is still investigating, so the media has been kept out of it," Tanner said. "People touted the Colorado town as the new Aspen, and the ski resorts would've brought in a thousand jobs. But after the fires, the developers moved to a less risky area."

"So now you think this group may have come here because the town is planning to expand the ski resort onto government land? Then, why suspect my father?" Another sickening thud hit her stomach. "You think he's a SOLO extremist? That's insane. He may have joined the organization to support their conservation efforts, like I'm sure many people have, but he'd never support the radical fringe." She groaned in frustration. "Their whole purpose doesn't make sense. Burn down the forest—kill trees and wildlife so people can't develop the land? Crazy!"

"Common sense doesn't stop people like them." He reached into his back pocket and withdrew a creased index card. "Did your father ever mention any of these individuals?"

She scanned the list. "I recognize some, but I can't believe any of these guys would be involved. My dad knew almost everyone in Pine Lake. Sure, he opposed the new ski resort in the beginning, but mainly because the runs were expanding into an area he cared about. But he'd never put his own personal beliefs above people's safety." She ran her finger over the section of the map where the hotel once stood. "You don't believe me."

"I believe in data, and right now the facts conflict."

Kitty pushed off the desk. "You want data? Fine. Let's get started then. There must be a clue somewhere in this mess." She wiped her cold hands on her jeans and scrutinized the piles of paper. "We have a lot to do."

"We?" He barked out a short, derisive laugh. "I'm sorry, there is no 'we.' The sheriff and I are still following up leads. I know it's hard, but you're just going to have to trust us to do our jobs." His tone softened. "Why don't you just go home to L.A., and I'll be in touch with you in a couple days."

She gazed out the window at the giant oak tree her father had refused to cut down to widen the parking area. It would be a relief to leave Pine Lake, but what would she tell her grandmother if they continued to believe her father was an arsonist? Kitty didn't trust Tanner or Sheriff Johnson to be as thorough as she.

"I'm going to stick around for a while."

Tanner frowned but didn't appear surprised. "Well, I can't force you to leave." He moved toward the door. "Just be careful."

"You're the second person to tell me that today. Do you think I might be in danger?"

"Don't you find it strange someone would call you about the case against your dad without identifying himself?"

"From this town? Are you kidding?" She laughed. "No offense, but an isolated place like this can attract odd people. You ask the Pine Lake residents why they moved to seven thousand feet where jobs are scarce and the nearest shopping mall is more than a hundred miles away, and you'll get as many different answers as there are acorns in the oak tree out there." She nodded meaningfully. "It takes effort to want to survive up here. A lot don't stick it out through the first winter."

Kitty scrutinized Tanner's strong profile as he straightened a stack on his desk. She didn't have any doubt that if this man wanted to stay in Pine Lake, he'd make it work. What was his story? Was he running away from something too?

"Just the same, watch your step. Don't give the sheriff a reason to nail you for obstructing justice."

Kitty grimaced. "Don't worry, he's not someone I want to spend time with." She ran her palm over the scarred desk. "I have a question. Do you know if the stuff in this desk was moved before last night?"

"Whatever wasn't confiscated as possible evidence is in my garage." Tanner glanced at his watch. "I didn't see anything valuable. Mostly paperwork. Letters, newspaper clippings, stuff like that. Why?"

Kitty chewed on her lower lip, debating whether to mention the notebooks, but she really wanted to read them before the sheriff and Tanner did. She shrugged. "You never know what might be useful."

"I'll get the boxes for you this afternoon." He glanced at his watch. "Now, if we're finished, I have to get to work."

Kitty hesitated by the dusty window as Tanner's footsteps faded into the bay. Near her Jeep, a pair of Steller's jays squabbled over a bug on the concrete. The wind shook the tree branches, and with a burst of dark-blue feathers, the birds flashed by and disappeared.

She sighed, a restless yearning filling her heart. Much as she enjoyed her fast-paced life in Los Angeles, she missed the wild beauty of the Sierras. The sound of the wind in the trees instead of the bustle of traffic. Wildlife consisting of animals rather than human predators on the streets. And sweet air she could breathe with carefree abandon and not have to check the smog levels on the morning news. Not that she'd ever consider moving back. Not after the way they'd treated her. Too many narrow-minded people, some supposedly Christians, who'd snubbed her because of her sullenness and her poor choice of friends.

Maybe she'd deserved their criticism. She'd been confused and hurt after her mother had dumped her in Pine Lake with a father she barely knew. She'd lashed out at her anger and frustration by running wild with the wrong crowd for a few years.

But weren't Christians supposed to forgive? Ten years spent living in Pine Lake and she'd felt like an outsider. Now, some of the same people were trying to smear her father's name. But they hadn't bested him in life, and she wouldn't let them succeed after his death.

With renewed determination, she marched into the garage. Tanner was dragging a fire hose across the floor to fold the length in half, a tedious routine she knew well. Fire hoses needed to be cleaned, dried and put away after each use.

She trotted to the opposite end, knelt and snapped the upper hose so it stayed aligned with the lower half as Tanner rolled it into a coil larger than a bicycle wheel.

"Thanks," he grunted. His shoulder bumped hers as the coil reached the brass fittings. He heaved the bundle onto a rack against the wall.

"This place needs a good scrubbing," she said and grabbed another hose from the pile on the floor.

"We're short-handed, and two structure fires last week didn't give us much time to clean up."

They continued to work in silence. Kitty's mind wandered. How long ago had Tanner's wife died? On their last day together, had Luke told his wife he loved her? Or did they part on angry words like she and her father?

She tugged her cell phone from her pocket. No messages. Not even a call from Nana. She glanced at Tanner. Did he ever feel lonely? Probably not, because his son and a father lived with him.

She steered her attention back to the chaos. However competent Tanner might've been on past jobs, obviously he was in over his head here.

"You need me." Her voice echoed off the metal walls. She sat back on her heels, stunned she'd spoken that aloud.

Tanner looked up from examining a dent in a brass coupling. "Excuse me?"

Kitty's cheeks warmed. "I mean, you could use some assistance." She sprang to her feet and pushed open the tall bay doors. Sunlight streamed in, exposing even more mud on the floor.

"You need someone to sort through the mess in the office and clean out here. I'm a trained firefighter, so you might as well put me to use."

"I can't just let anyone handle those papers. There's confidential medical information in there."

She held up a hand. "Don't worry—I worked here. Because I was just a paid-call employee, I bet Dad never removed me from the books. You can check, assuming you can find the personnel files. I'm legit."

She yanked on a skinny water hose dangling from a pipe in the ceiling. She aimed the nozzle at the muddy concrete. The water stream hit a puddle of motor oil, and Tanner jumped before it splashed onto his boots and jeans.

"Sorry, but please pay attention." Kitty released the handle. "Admit it, what I said makes sense. We can help each other."

"Maybe I don't want your help."

She shrugged with indifference even though her pulse raced. "You might as well let me try. Otherwise, I'll just have to tag around after you until I get what I need."

"That's harassment," he said harshly, but the corners of his mouth twitched.

"Maybe." She shrugged again and focused on washing ash and sludge off a long, beige hose. After several minutes passed, she blew out an impatient breath, ruffling her bangs. "Well?"

She turned and found herself alone. "Tanner?"

"I guess we could work out something."

Startled, Kitty looked up to find him standing on the engine bed. He swung down beside her. "You won't like working for me."

Yes! She wanted to leap with victory, but she merely nodded. "I'll survive."

"I'm going to go fill out the duty roster for next week, and then I have some business in town." He tossed a dingy sponge at her. "You can wash the engines. That ought to keep you out of trouble until I get back."

Kitty picked up the sponge and wrinkled her nose as Tanner headed into the office. She would rather sort the files, searching for clues. Scrubbing the three fire engines and the brush truck would take at least two hours to do a proper job, but right now wasn't the time to rock the boat. She was in. Ironic, though, because a few years ago she'd been dying to get out.

A siren blasted through the station. She ran toward the office in time to hear a female voice from the county Communication Center. "Station 169, Fire Investigation. Smoke reported on the south ridge below Pine Lake. Forest Service has been notified. Please verify."

Tanner snatched up the radio mic. Kitty turned, raced out

the bay doors and jumped into the driver's seat of the red Bronco parked outside. She fired up the engine.

Tanner tapped on the window. He motioned at her to move, and when she wouldn't budge, he yanked the door open. "Out!"

"I'm going. You just hired me, remember?"

His jaw tightened.

"I know a back way down the ridge. I can save you fifteen minutes," she added.

"Move over." He climbed in, his hard hip assisting her slide across the squeaky vinyl to the passenger side. Flipping on the red lights, he stomped on the pedal. Tires squealed as they shot out of the parking lot. "You've been an employee for what? Ten minutes? And you already think you can do whatever you want. I give the orders. You obey if you ever want to set foot inside the station again. Got it?"

"Yes, sir!" Kitty pulled on her seatbelt instead of saluting. He'd probably toss her from the car without bothering to slow down if he knew what she thought about his "orders."

They sped south of town. Kitty looked out her window to where the ground fell sharply away from the two-lane road before leveling out to a plateau and then plunged down a series of small canyons. A minuscule puff of smoke drifted skyward.

"Stop!" she yelled. Tanner jerked the steering wheel. The truck skidded off the pavement, spewing up a billow of dust. Kitty pointed at the faint haze far below them. "Down there. Smoke's coming from the Fish Creek area."

Tanner peered through his binoculars, looking grim. "The campground is supposed to be closed because of the fire danger." He handed the binoculars to Kitty. Even with the magnification maxed out, she couldn't pinpoint the source.

"The old logging road is fifty yards up on the right. See the marker lying on the ground?"

"Hang on." Tanner shifted into four-wheel drive and plowed through brush before landing on the tire tracks that plummeted down the hill. Kitty clamped her rattling teeth together as they bounced over the ruts and washed-out gullies.

After two steep miles, they reached the two metal pipes marking the back entrance to the Fish Creek Camp. The chain gate snaked across the ground, and Tanner drove over it. A bluish haze hung over the clearing, but the small campground appeared deserted. The truck jerked to a stop. Kitty jumped out and ran to where the smoke seemed the thickest. Green pine branches smoldered over hot coals in a fire ring. The pungent smoke billowed about in the breeze, stinging her eyes and nose.

Tanner strode up, speaking into his handheld radio, giving their position to the Forest Service. Kitty scrambled up on a large boulder to get a better view. "Nothing but a campfire," she reported. "All this will entail is issuing a ticket."

Tanner snapped the radio into his belt holder. "To who? You see anyone?"

Kitty squinted in the bright sunlight, still scanning the area. "Nope. But they can't be far. Those branches haven't been burning long."

"Of all the stupid, irresponsible things to do. There are signs posted all around here warning against fires. One good wind and the whole mountain could go up in flames unless—"

"Unless that was their intention," She finished for him, her stomach knotting. Her gaze swept the ridge. No dust clouds betrayed any moving vehicles. "We're south of town, and the wind's blowing north."

"Doesn't make sense they used the campground. If this were another arson attempt, why build a fire in the fire ring and attract attention by using green wood?"

"Who knows? Maybe they wanted to make it look like an accident. I'll get the shovel." Kitty trotted to the Bronco and dug the shovel out from under the piled equipment. She raced back to Tanner, panting in the oxygen-thin air.

She leaned against a tree to catch her breath as Tanner deftly extinguished the flames. Muscles rippled under his white shirt and a sooty shaft of sunlight struck his hair, making the waves gleam like polished black marble. He reminded her of a soldier on a mission. Confident and determined in the face of danger.

"You all right?"

"Huh?" She blinked, mortified that he'd caught her staring at him again. What was wrong with her? She'd come back from L.A. to prove what fools Tanner and the sheriff were being about her father. This man was supposed to be the enemy, but she kept acting like a schoolgirl with a crush.

Tanner frowned, still watching her. "Is the altitude bothering you?"

"Maybe," she said, although she realized less oxygen wasn't the only cause of her racing heart. Tanner was dangerous to her in more ways than just destroying her father's memory.

She nodded in the direction of the campground entrance. "Isn't the gate supposed to be locked?"

"Someone cut the padlock." He threw another dirt load and smoke rose in a swirling cloud.

"No signs anyone's pitched a tent here recently."

"Most likely it was kids fooling around." He stomped out the last burning ember. "They like to come down here to party."

"Yes, I know," Kitty said. She'd been part of that crowd before she'd smartened up and realized her ticket to freedom and out of Pine Lake wouldn't come from carousing and landing in jail.

Tanner shot her an assessing glance before scanning the campground again. "We better look around before I call in an all clear."

They separated and she scouted the east end where giant boulders and dense, thorny chaparral hemmed the campground. The wind had blown most of the heavy smoke from the campfire northward, but a dusky fog floated above a shallow ravine that dropped steeply away from the last campsite. Kitty skidded down the embankment. Gray wisps seeped out of the ground by a fallen log. She dug through the pine needles to discover a small hole. A steady ribbon of smoke streamed out.

Scrambling back up the hill, Kitty shouted, "Tanner, over here." She waved her arms until he caught sight of her.

"Look at this," she said after he joined her. She shoved the log over with her boot. Smoke billowed up through crannies in the rocky earth. Tanner used the shovel and unearthed a smoldering pile of twigs and dried leaves.

"Careful," he warned as Kitty squatted and lifted a tin can out of a small pile of rocks. "Smells like lighter fluid." She set the cylinder gently to the side.

"The log is soaked with something, too. Pretty clever delay device. Keep an eye on it. I have to go radio the sheriff. I can't get a signal in the ravine. Here, blow this if you sense any trouble." He handed her a whistle and climbed to the camp area.

Kitty spent the next several minutes systematically scouting the area as they'd trained her in class. No dropped litter, except a rusty soda can. Not even the baked ground revealed any tracks. No clues at all.

The minutes ticked by, and smoke curled from the log again. *Arson.* The thought sent alternating waves of fear and excitement through her. The same maniac who set the Wildcat Ravine could've struck again, which would prove her father innocent. But it also meant he could still out there, waiting to strike again.

The trees and brush grew too high up on the walls to provide much shade, and hot rays beat down on her head. Wisps of hair escaped her ponytail and stuck to her neck along with gritty dust, making her skin itch. She shooed away the tiny black gnats buzzing around her face as a pebble bounced down on the opposite ravine wall. Then another. Something moved along the ridge.

Clutching the shovel, she climbed the ravine edge, but she still couldn't see over the dense chaparral thicket. Dry vegetation crunched. Her pulse quickened. Could it be an animal foraging for food? Or…had the arsonist returned to the scene of the crime?

She waved at Tanner, who stood by the truck, still conversing on the radio. He glanced in her direction and held up a finger, indicating he needed a minute. Behind her, the rustling noise grew fainter. She didn't have a minute, and she couldn't use the whistle he'd given her. By the time Tanner got here, whoever roamed back there would disappear.

As quietly as possible, Kitty jammed the shovel deep into the thick wall of thorny bush. Leaning forward, she could almost see through the leaves to the other side. Just another six inches and…was that a blue shirt? The shovel jerked, yanking her forward. She pitched over a rock and fell into the bush.

"Tanner!" Kitty yelled and inhaled dust. She coughed as she struggled to stand. The shovel was gone. Through the foliage, a shape loomed toward her. She backed away, but the long thorns caught her hair.

Gritting her teeth, she wrenched herself free as the steel shovel crashed through the branches. She ducked, but the metal grazed her head, knocking her sideways into the ravine. Sound and light exploded before everything went black.

Luke glanced at the stoic woman sitting beside him in the Bronco. Her face averted, she hadn't said a word since they'd started the hour-long trip back from the Butler hospital. With her feet planted on the seat and arms wrapped rigidly around her legs, her body language indicated she was still steamed.

"If you don't relax, you'll have a stiff neck to go along with the bump on your head," he said gently.

Kitty shot him a scathing look.

"Hey, I already apologized, and in partial penance, I filled out a million hospital forms for you. What more do you want?"

She turned away again.

He gripped the steering wheel hard and swung the truck around a hairpin curve. He wasn't sure who to be angrier with at the moment—the McGuire woman or himself. Even if she shouldn't have investigated on her own, full responsibility for the incident fell on him. First, he hadn't taken enough precautions to make sure he'd cleared the area of possible danger. Second, he should've never left her alone, and third, he'd been out of his mind to hire her.

His chest still burned at the memory of Kitty lying on the ground, her face pale and still beneath the tangled golden curls. For one frightening minute, he'd thought she was dead. And she might be in the morgue right now if, as his dad would say, her guardian angel hadn't been working overtime.

Luke believed in God's protection, but God also gave humans brains and expected them to use them to take care of themselves. In this case, he was thankful God had stepped in. Just as He had with Michael.

The heartburn flamed up his throat. As an FBI agent, he'd seen his share of violent crime, but during his son's kidnapping, it had been almost impossible to remain focused and objective. Every minute of every day had been filled with guilt and grief. If he hadn't been five minutes late picking up Michael after soccer practice, Michael wouldn't have been out on the street and tricked into a madman's car.

The nine months of waiting for news or a lead had been almost unbearable. Sometimes, late at night, Luke still woke in a sweat, plagued by the helpless terror he'd felt the two times he'd gone to the city morgue for a John Doe fitting Michael's description. Would it be his son lying on that cold stainless steel table? Then came the elation, followed by the guilty shame at his joy when another set of parents would be grieving. It'd taken every shred of faith he had left to survive the ordeal, and he had, barely. Miranda hadn't been so lucky.

If only Miranda had hung on a little longer and not let grief eat her up. After her death, they'd discovered the kidnapper's name. Jim Sorenson. Luke had put Sorenson's embezzling son behind bars. Through a glitch in the system, Sorenson had tracked Luke down and in an act of revenge, had grabbed Michael. Thankfully, Sorenson hadn't physically harmed Michael, but he'd tried to brainwash Michael against his father and at times, Luke felt like Sorenson had succeeded.

His knuckles ached, and he loosened his hold on the steering wheel. The past might forever haunt Michael, but they'd made progress building a new life. His son was worth it all: Quitting the Bureau, leaving Chicago for this secluded town, joining the local church and even attending the long, tedious PTA meetings that would've sent weaker men screaming into the backcountry.

If only Michael would trust him and not fight him at every turn. The counselor said if they didn't have a breakthrough soon, there might never be one. Time was slipping away.

He should've never taken on the job as fire chief, even temporarily, but the sheriff decided it would arouse less suspicion among the locals if he helped investigate in an official capacity. So had the FBI taskforce assigned to work on SOLO. He couldn't quit now, not with the danger still out there.

Please, God, help me solve this case before it's too late to salvage a good relationship with Michael.

"Are you okay?" Kitty asked with a frown.

"Ah, the woman speaks at last," he said, seeing her wince as the Bronco bounced onto the narrow road leading to Pine Lake.

"The pills the doctor gave you will help the pain if you'd just take them," he offered. Kitty lifted her chin in a defiant move, and he grinned despite his bad mood. She had spunk. "You don't have to be so obstinate. Accidents happen. Everyone gets hurt sometimes, especially in our line of work."

"I don't," she declared and then grabbed her head as the tires rocked over a pothole. "At least, not too often. Besides, this wasn't an accident."

He nodded grimly. "All the more reason for you to go home."

"I'm not scared off this easily. The arsonist is still out there, and this proves my dad didn't set the Wildcat fire."

If only it could be that simple. He sighed. "Or it could mean his accomplices are still around—and dangerous."

She stared out the window to the valley below. The glow from the sunset danced over her, firing up the brassy streaks in her blond locks, the same bright tint of his son's downy hair as a baby.

Michael.

He glanced at his watch as tension knotted in his neck. He'd called his father about the delay, and they were either eating at Sarah's Café, or maybe Elizabeth had cooked. Once again, he'd missed dinner with his son. More time lost.

Was he ever going to be the kind of father he wanted to be?

FOUR

The sun had disappeared behind the western mountain range by the time Luke parked in front of the McGuire cabin and killed the engine.

"We're here," he informed Kitty, who'd closed her eyes and remained quiet for the remainder of the trip. She blinked and straightened, brushing back her tangled hair.

Lights from his home on the hill beckoned to him. "I assume you didn't find other accommodations this morning. Is there someone who can stay with you tonight?"

She shook her head. "The doctor said I'd be fine."

"Yeah, in a few days. He wanted to keep you in the hospital overnight for observation."

"And you're listening as well as he did. I'm okay, all right?" she said through clenched teeth as she climbed out of the cab.

"Sure you are," he muttered as he got out of the truck. The weathered porch creaked beneath their weight and a nail head scratched his boot. He ran his hand over peeling paint on the railing. "This porch could use some work before someone falls through. You have dry rot."

"Correction, the town council has dry rot since they're repossessing the place." She waited for him to unlock the door. "Anything else you want to criticize before I turn in?"

Luke sighed. "Take the keys—you can give them to me later. I also had Daniel Moore fix the window, so you should be more secure."

She arched her delicate eyebrows. "Thank you."

He hesitated. "You have anything to eat in there?"

"Don't worry. I'm a big girl. I can take care of myself."

He held his hands up in surrender and stepped away. Fine. If she didn't want his help, he couldn't do anything about it. The sheriff could send a deputy patrol to check on her later. Or better yet, arrest her and take her in so they could watch her.

He glanced up at the darkening sky and grimaced. Oh, who was he kidding? Once he got Michael settled for the night, he'd return to check on her. His conscience wouldn't let him do anything less.

Luke paused by the truck as she opened the door. She shrieked and stumbled back onto the porch. He charged up the steps. "What is it?"

"Some—someone's in there. I mean—"

"Stay here." He pushed her upright against the wall and automatically reached behind his back before he remembered he didn't carry his gun anymore. He'd locked the weapon in a box the day he quit the FBI and moved to Pine Lake.

He picked up a splintered chair leg, quickly scanning the cabin's decimated interior for any movement. He checked the kitchen and then the two bedrooms. Someone had tossed all the rooms, but the culprit was gone. Anger mounted in his gut as he returned to the living room where Kitty unsteadily picked books off the floor.

"Leave them," he commanded, and then lowered his voice when she cringed. "The sheriff will want to see the place the way we found it."

She dropped the books, and he read shocked disbelief in her eyes as she took in the damage. Cottony filler puffed from gaping holes in the chairs and sofa, and jagged knife cuts ran like rivers across the coffee table's aged pine. Shelf contents lay scattered and smashed. Drawers dumped.

"Did you actually see someone when you came in?" he asked.

She shook her head, and then gasped as she pointed to a splintered painting jammed into the stone fireplace. The iron fireplace poker jabbed through the canvas where Sam McGuire's face should've been.

Kitty doubled over, clutching her stomach. Luke helped her outside and cradled her head against his chest. "It's okay. They're only things. No one was hurt."

"P-please leave me alone for a second."

He let his fingers slip away from the silky curls as she leaned weakly on the railing. Her long limbs trembled. "That does it, we're going back to the hospital," he said, pulling the keys from his pocket.

"Don't be ridiculous." She swayed upright and steadied herself. "I just had the wind knocked out of me."

The woman didn't look all right to him. He'd seen this expression many times before: shock warring with denial and fear.

The skin on her face seemed almost translucent, making her spattering of freckles pop out darkly across the bridge of her nose. But at least her breathing had slowed to a normal rate and judging by the determined set to her mouth and squared shoulders, she'd put up a fight if he tried to drag her back into the truck. He didn't relish wasting another hour driving to Butler if she refused to let him admit her to the hospital again.

One thing was for certain, she couldn't stay here. He rubbed his aching neck. "Okay, we're going to leave everything the way we found it. I'll radio for the sheriff, and then you're coming to my house for the night." He nearly bit his tongue. Why had he offered his home? Surely, he could find someone else to take her in.

"Why?" she said, echoing his thoughts.

"Why? Because whoever tossed this place might return. The bedroom window is smashed in this time."

"I don't think it's a good idea." Her lips puckered as if she tasted something sour.

Annoyance flooded him. The woman made it clear she didn't have a high opinion of him, but she could at least show some gratitude.

"This isn't personal. I'm not making a pass at you…my son and father will be there."

Her face reddened. "This is *my* problem, Tanner. Just call the sheriff and I'll wait for him."

Luke jammed his fists into his pockets. *Lord, grant me patience.*

"Listen here, McGuire, you've been uncooperative all day, and I'm too tired to deal with it anymore. You insisted on going on the call, refused to ride in the ambulance, hassled the emergency room doctor and now you want to argue with me. You have a *head injury.* You could lapse into unconsciousness, and no one would know about it. Enough is enough." He glowered down at her. "If you want to be involved any further in this investigation, then you have to listen to what I tell you. Neither of us may like it, but the moment you accompanied me on the call, I became responsible for you."

She glared at him, her eyes glittering like cold sapphires under the porch light. He stared back, daring her to defy him. "Maybe we should go visit the sheriff, and you can spend a night in a cell. The beds are quite comfortable, from what I hear. At least I'll have peace of mind knowing you're not alone."

"Are you always this stubborn?" she asked with a small smile.

"Yep."

Her rigid shoulders relaxed. "Okay, you win. I'll go. But just for tonight." She marched down the stairs to the Bronco. "You said you were going to get the boxes with my dad's things for me too, remember? Now would be a good time for us to go through them."

He smothered a grin and followed her. He should've guessed she had an ulterior motive when she gave in. She was the one of the most aggravating women he'd ever met, but he couldn't help but admire her audacity.

He called the sheriff's office as they drove up the hill to his place. Kitty listened quietly as he finished talking to the deputy on call, her hands clenched as they rolled into his driveway, betraying her unease. A longing to comfort her swept over him, to assure her everything would be all right, but it would be a lie.

"How long have you lived here?" she asked, staring at the rambling building shadowed by the black oak trees lining the ridge.

"I've only been here about six months, my father a year longer."

"It looks bigger than I remember."

"That's because we're adding on an apartment. My father will live in the addition," he explained as Kitty trailed him to the porch.

She glanced around them. "Where's your dog?"

"Jack stays with my son, Michael, most of the time." He punched the code into the alarm system and shoved the door open. Automatic timers had already filled the wide, high-beamed living room with soft light.

Kitty gestured to the table saw and pile of tools in the entryway. "Still remodeling?"

"Some." He followed her gaze around the drastically altered space. With his father's help, he'd knocked out the walls between the kitchen, living room and dining area to make an open, airy floor plan. After stripping away the aged wallpaper, they'd re-varnished the cedar paneling until it glowed in the spot lighting. Finally and most importantly, he'd replaced the outside wall adjacent to the deck with sliding glass doors. During the day, the majesty of the snow-covered peaks and the sky rushed into the room and melded with the rustic decor.

Kitty's boots sank into the smoky blue Navaho rug as she meandered to the vast stone fireplace and drank in the room's earth-and-sky colors. She tossed back her hair, freed from the ponytail, as she studied the painting of the Four Sisters hanging over the mantle. She turned with a smile. "I'm impressed. This place looks great."

Luke cleared his throat, trying to ignore how much he liked the warm approval in her voice. "Thanks. Remodeling has always been a hobby of mine. I finally got serious enough about it to get a contractor's license. When this case is wrapped up, I'll have time to finish the place." He'd also hoped by working together on the house, he'd get Michael interested in something other than video games, but so far it hadn't worked. The kid still snuck off to his bedroom every chance he got.

He trudged down the two steps to the sunken living area and picked up a shiny wooden apple his father had whittled. He tossed the globe back and forth between his hands as Kitty walked to the window and gazed out. "How are you feeling?"

She flicked a glance his way. "If I lapse into a coma, I'll let you know."

"It would be funny if it weren't a possibility," he said dryly. "The bathroom is down the hall on the left if you want to clean up."

"A hot shower would feel great, but…." Her smudged face turned down to examine her torn, dirt-encrusted clothing. "I should've grabbed my bag. I wasn't thinking when we left the cabin."

That made two of them. He sighed. "I need to run back down and meet the sheriff. What do you need?"

"Just the green duffel bag on the couch. At least that's where I left it." Painful confusion flashed in her eyes before she looked away. "Maybe I should go with you."

"No, you've had enough for today. I'll get the duffel bag. Tomorrow you can go check to see if anything is missing. I'll only be gone a few minutes." He strode to the door. "My father and son are probably at the church and won't be back for a couple hours. If you need anything, push the speed dial on the phone to connect to my cell. Help yourself to any food in the kitchen."

He was pulling the door shut when Kitty's voice stopped him.

"Luke?"

He blinked. She'd used his first name, and to his surprise, he liked the sound.

"Don't forget to get my dad's stuff out of the garage."

He rolled his eyes. "Right, of course." He tried to close the door, but her hand curved around the frame. "Stay inside and rest."

"Luke?"

"What?" He sighed with exasperation. They'd spent more than an hour in the truck, but *now* she wanted to talk?

"Thank you," she whispered and stretched upward on tiptoe. Her soft lips brushed his cheek. Before he could react, the door closed in his face.

* * *

Kitty plopped on the leather couch, already regretting her impulsive action. What must Luke Tanner be thinking? She touched her lips where they'd met his prickly, very masculine evening shadow. Nothing wrong with being grateful, was there? Luke had rescued her back at the camp and then amazingly stuck by her all afternoon, even when she'd been rude to him and everyone else.

Maybe the knock on the head had addled her brain, but she liked how his name formed on her tongue. "Luke," she tested the name aloud and then bit her lower lip. *Stop it!* Her emotions were on overload and she was entering dangerous territory.

She lifted the cedar apple from the side table. Polished to a high sheen, the wood felt silky smooth and still held heat from Luke's hands, the same warmth that had caressed her face when she'd awakened on the ground. She groaned and set it back down.

Why was this happening now? She hadn't expected Luke Tanner or any man to ever stir such an intense yearning again. She didn't want any romantic entanglements in her life. Not after watching her parents' disastrous marriage explode, and certainly not after her failed engagement to Jordan. Some people, especially those with risky jobs, needed to be detached and independent to succeed. Not be distracted like she was now.

Maybe this wasn't a good idea to stay here. Sarah would let her bunk in her guest bedroom, but Kitty always felt uncomfortable in her elaborately decorated house. Besides, Sarah couldn't mind her own business. She'd call Kitty's grandmother and tell Nana that Kitty had gotten hurt. She'd done it in the past, and Kitty didn't want to worry Nana.

She set the apple back by a worn-looking black Bible on the side table. The leather cover lay open exposing the inscription.

Luke,
I hope you find the strength I did in this Book. May you always live up to the goodness found here. Happy 12th birthday.
Love, Dad.

A familiar ache seeped into her heart. The divorce had been rough. She'd only been five and couldn't understand why her father didn't come home anymore. Her mother had given her a Bible and taken Kitty to church for the six years they lived alone together in L.A. They had changed addresses frequently, so Kitty never did become ensconced in any one congregation.

Then one day her mother announced she was going to start a new life with a new man in a new state. She'd dropped Kitty in Pine Lake and promised she'd be back soon. It took Kitty about a year before she figured out her mother had lied. Her father tried to explain that leaving people and problems behind was a pattern in her mother's life, and Kitty shouldn't take it personally.

Personally? How else could she take it? Her mother had left her only child without a backward glance. Kitty had blamed herself and lashed out in the only way she knew how, by pushing people away or hanging with troubled kids who were running from problems, too.

Her father didn't know how to handle her and continued to drop her off at the community church each week, probably hoping they'd be a good influence with his wayward daughter. But over the years, Kitty's attendance declined until she couldn't remember the last time she went to a service.

Church ceased to be important in her daily life, or maybe it had been the other way around. The church never cared much for her.

But there was no sense in dwelling in the past; she had a case to solve. She focused on the titles of the the books underneath the Bible. Most of books were basic firefighting and first aid instruction manuals, apparently new, judging from the barely cracked spines.

Sticking out of one was the familiar county certificate of completion for a basic firefighting and first responder class dated two months ago. Strange. The law required firefighters to have refresher courses every year, but this was a first-time certification. Sure, Pine Lake only had a paid call department, but why hadn't the town council hired someone with more experience for fire chief? Someone like Daniel Moore, or some of the other old-timers who'd been with the department for years.

She sighed and rubbed her aching shoulder. Maybe she shouldn't jump to conclusions. There could be a perfectly good explanation, like Luke might be certified in another state and gone back for a complete course. She'd have to ask Evan if he knew anything about this.

What was taking Luke so long? Kitty wandered out onto the redwood deck and gazed down at her father's cabin. Light beamed from the windows. The Bronco and a squad car were still parked in the driveway. Had they found something vital to her father's case? Time to call Luke and see what was going on.

As she reached the sliding door, a faint scraping sound, like fingernails on a blackboard, shot chills along her spine. Her gaze darted over the deck. The leaves, high on the towering oaks, quivered, but the looming shadows remained motionless, mocking her apprehension.

She stepped inside, and a thud shook the floor. Kitty

shrieked and fumbled for the switch, flooding the area with light. A giant Coulter pinecone lay rocking on the deck. She pressed her hand over her thumping heart as a hysterical giggle tickled her throat. She'd been away so long from the mountains, she'd forgotten about nature's foot-long missiles.

She hefted the pinecone into a lounge chair so no one would trip on it and headed for the phone again. A loud creak shot across the ceiling. She stared at the beams. Another creak reverberated.

Had the wind picked up, causing the beams to groan or… was someone on the roof? Were those footsteps? Her heart pounded again, as the sound moved across the ceiling toward the entryway. Silence stretched, and a thud hit the porch. Kitty snatched up the phone as the doorknob on the front door rattled and stilled. She gasped. Surely Luke had thrown the lock. The knob rattled again, but this time the door inched open.

No time to call for help. She grabbed a hammer lying on the table saw. "Hey! What do you think you're doing?" she shouted, slamming the door against the wall.

A woman screamed and dropped her grocery bag, the contents flying across the porch. Kitty staggered back and dropped the hammer. "Oh…I'm so sorry. I thought—"

What had she thought? Footsteps! Kitty pushed past the frightened woman and ran down the steps. The floodlights obscured her vision, but only shingles occupied the steep, slanted roof. She ran to the side where the eave hung about six or seven feet from the high rock cutout against the mountain. Risky, but someone might be able leap to the rooftop if he was determined enough.

"Did you see anyone on the roof?"

The woman shook her head, staring wide-eyed at Kitty as if she were crazy.

"It's probably just a dumb old squirrel," a boy with a back-pack slung over his shoulder said, hopping out of minivan parked in the driveway. He shot Kitty a disdainful look.

Tangled, copper-colored hair hung over eyes the same dark color as Luke's. He couldn't be more than ten or eleven years old, but the belligerent tone in his voice aged him. Jack jumped out of the car, his golden eyes surveying the sur-roundings. The dog circled the kid and then sat, its unfriendly gaze fixed on Kitty.

"Michael, come here. Now." The woman pressed a cell phone to her ear and inched toward the door. The boy dragged a toe of his tennis shoe through the dirt, ignoring her.

"If you're calling the sheriff, say hi from me. He already knows I'm here," Kitty said, hoping to calm the woman. The last thing she needed was another conversation with the sheriff. Somehow, he'd probably find a way to blame her for what happened to the cabin.

"I'm really sorry I scared you," she continued. "You must think I'm insane. I'm Kitty McGuire. I used to live in Pine Lake, and I'm…temporarily working with Luke. He should be back any minute." She gestured to the portable phone lying in the doorway. "In fact, I was trying to call him when—"

"McGuire? Oh, yes." The woman glanced at the fire department emblem on Kitty's shirt and snapped her cell shut. "Sarah said Sam's daughter was in town." She quivered for a moment like a sparrow settling her feathers and offered her small hand with manicured nails. "I'm Elizabeth Greene, friend of the family."

Kitty shook Elizabeth's hand. Not one glossy, brunette strand of hair framing her fine-featured face seemed out of place, and her neat denim skirt and jacket appeared as crisp as if she'd just whisked the outfit off an ironing board. Kitty felt even more grimy and disheveled. She sighed. Where was Luke with her clean clothes?

"You're staying *here?*" the boy asked, his eyes narrowing.

"Yes," Kitty said, narrowing her gaze back at him. "Just for tonight. Is that a problem?"

His scowl deepened. "Don't touch my PlayStation."

"Michael Jason Tanner, you mind your manners," Elizabeth scolded.

Michael whipped around. "You're not my mother. You can't tell me what to do!" He stomped up the stairs and into the house. Jack trotted after him.

"I apologize for his rudeness." Elizabeth bent to gather the torn paper bag of groceries, pink infusing her plump cheeks. "That's Luke's son, and he had a rough day at school."

"I'm edgy myself." Kitty picked up the hammer lying in the doorway. "It's been a rough day all around. Someone ransacked my father's cabin. Luke is down there with the sheriff."

Elizabeth nearly dropped her armload of produce. "Oh, how awful. I don't understand what's happening around here. Break-ins. Vandalism. Fires. It's unbelievable. Was anyone hurt?" Her gaze shifted to the small bandage on Kitty's forehead.

Kitty hesitated, not sure how to answer. Getting knocked on the head was embarrassing. Here she'd come home as a tough, savvy firefighter and ended up at the hospital her first day. She didn't know what this woman would do with the information. Not that Elizabeth looked like a troublemaker, but one never knew. Her friend, Sarah, was a perfect example. The café owner appeared to be the sweet, motherly, great-aunt type, but in reality she was a savvy businesswoman with an iron will. Plus, she could be one of the biggest gossips in Pine Lake. If someone had any secrets, it was best not to confide in Sarah.

"I wasn't home at the time," Kitty finally said.

"What a relief. With the recent burglaries and then the

fire danger being so high, everyone's nerves are stretched thin. Sometimes Pine Lake doesn't seem like a safe haven anymore."

Was it ever safe? Kitty pondered, as she followed Elizabeth into the house. Maybe security was just an illusion. For what had really changed over the years? She and her friends had been adept at breaking and entering, not that she ever personally stole anything. She just liked the adrenaline rush of seeing if she could do it, and she quit before the offenses escalated. Most of her cohorts, who hadn't ended up in jail, had eventually bailed for more populated areas. Still, if all the recent events were connected, then the culprit probably had lived here for a while. Someone who knew the citizens and area well. Someone she or her father might've even known.

"I should've recognized you from Sam's funeral. God rest his soul," Elizabeth said. "My heartfelt condolences. I got to know him quite well, considering I only moved here a year and half ago." She set the grocery bag on the kitchen counter. "I own Lizzy's Cards and Crafts on Main Street in the building next to the *Tribune* office. Sam inspected the smoke detectors, but we socialized at church."

Church? Kitty blinked. "We're talking about Sam *McGuire,* right?"

Elizabeth paused from her bustle around the kitchen, a can of corn in her hand. "Yes. Why?"

"It's just…church and my father don't compute." She tapped her temple.

Elizabeth laughed. "Well, I don't know about the past, but Sam and I belonged to the same weekly Bible study group."

Kitty stared at her, bewildered. Church? Bible study? Maybe she didn't know her father as well as she thought. If her dad had kept a major lifestyle change, such as attending church from her, then what other secrets had the man harbored?

"It's too risky," Luke said to the sheriff as they watched Evan Stone photograph the McGuire cabin's interior.

Johnson stuck his thumbs in his front pocket and leaned against the porch railing. "Which part? Encouraging Miss McGuire to remain in town? Or letting her help in the investigation? She may be useful. She did stop a potential forest fire this afternoon." He smirked. "What were *you* doing?"

Luke's stomach churned. "Hey, I never claimed to be good at this. As I recall, taking the job was *your* idea."

"I thought going undercover came second nature to you boys."

"Sorry to disillusion you. I may have worked for the Criminal Investigative Division, but the criminals I investigated didn't have any false pretense of my identity," Luke said. Besides, no one could fake being a fire chief for long. Despite his crash course in training, half the time he felt totally incompetent.

"Won't be for much longer."

"That's what you said two weeks ago. We'd be done by now if your team hadn't mucked up the investigation. I'd get back to my contracting business and spending more time with my son. You could've had your retirement party and been on your way to Montana to fly fish."

Johnson's features tightened into granite. "Seems we both have reasons to wrap this up quick."

Luke frowned. He shouldn't be taking his frustration out on the sheriff. They had the same goal in mind: keeping the town safe. "If McGuire remains in Pine Lake, we run the risk of setting her up as bait. I think it'd be best to convince her to return to L.A. If she's implicated, the authorities can pick her up there."

"Well, good luck on getting her to leave." Johnson snorted. "I've known the girl most of her life, and she's going to do what she wants to do. She arrived here with a huge chip on her shoulder and ran with the troublemakers. Caught her in a few pranks, like painting the founding father's statue purple and toilet papering the mayor's house, but when the big stuff went down with her friends for theft and drug possession, she managed to slip through the cracks."

"So she doesn't have a juvie record?"

Johnson shook his head. "I hauled her in a couple times, but somehow she never got officially booked. Couldn't find proof enough. Wouldn't even squeal on her friends, even when it looked like she'd take the fall for them." His stern features softened. "Guess I felt sorry for her. She was a little thing—about the age of your son—when her mother dumped her with Sam, who at that point was almost a stranger to her. Sam didn't know how to parent, and she ran wild. Poor kid."

"So you do have a heart under that badge." Luke grinned. "Who would've thought?"

Johnson scowled. "Doesn't stop me from doing my job. I'll arrest her without a moment's hesitation if I find any evidence she's involved. Her loyalty to her pack of friends almost caused her downfall, and it may be true in this case too." His gaze shifted back to the destroyed cabin interior. "Old habits die hard. She could be lying to cover for her father or came back here to get his piece of the pie."

"What pie?" Luke said more to himself than the sheriff. "We don't know what the perp was looking for."

Johnson spat over the railing. "Someone could've paid

Sam off in a number of ways. Cash, jewels, drugs, gold coins...."

Luke rubbed his chin. "I'd rule out large amounts of cash. We searched this place several times. From the way everything's torn up, it had to be something small. We could get a narc dog to come up and run through the place, but there's no indication Sam dealt drugs. Maybe we'll get a hit with the fingerprints."

At least, Luke hoped so. They were out of leads. Whether Sam was paid to set the fires himself or cover up for another arsonist, the money in his accounts came from someone. Most likely someone connected to SOLO.

He didn't like using Kitty as bait, even if it was the next logical step. Maybe a few years ago he might've justified using a civilian on the job, but he just couldn't stomach it anymore. "I still hate the idea of using Kitty. If that shovel hit her a few inches to the left, we wouldn't be having this conversation."

"Then, like I said, keep an eye on her. Way I figure it, whether she's naive or guilty of covering up for her father, she's still involved. Since she's going to hang around anyway, then we use it to our advantage. She can't stand me, so you'll have to stick close." He chuckled deep in his chest. "Shouldn't be too hard on you. She's grown up into a pretty thing. Firefighting has kept her fit."

Luke raised his eyebrows.

"What?" Johnson snorted. "Just because I've been married for a thousand years doesn't mean I don't notice an attractive woman. Watch her, though. She tends to jump before looking."

"So I've observed," Luke said, trying not to smile. Kitty's enthusiasm was contagious, and reminded him of himself in his early days with the bureau. He hadn't felt that passionate about a work-related cause since the day before Michael disappeared.

He fidgeted impatiently as Evan moved to the front bedroom, the windows flashing like sheet lightning. He would've rather waited until tomorrow for a state professional instead of this sarcastic, burned-out photojournalist, but in the interest of time, the sheriff had called Stone.

"Where are we on tracking down the cash flow Sam used to pay for the fancy nursing home his mother is in?" Johnson asked.

"Alec's still running background checks from the Bureau office. None of the money seems to have been filtered to Kitty. Her salary barely supports her and the high rent in L.A. I don't know how she's going to manage when she finds out they've frozen her father's trust fund for her grandmother."

"Not our problem." Johnson nodded toward the window. "Looks like Stone's done. Don't know what took him so long. I'm not paying him to stand around." He strode inside.

"I'll check in with you in the morning," Luke called after him as he carefully maneuvered down the groaning stairs. He'd get some planks tomorrow and hammer them over the rotten ones. No sense in having someone break their neck.

Luke jumped into the Bronco and fired up the engine. He'd already been down here forty-five minutes longer than planned. He gazed at the hill. Light gleamed from the attic window, which meant Michael was home.

He turned the truck down the dirt road. Despite Luke's misgiving, Johnson was right. Kitty seemed determined to stay in Pine Lake until they ruled out Sam as a suspect. Because that wasn't likely going to happen, he was stuck with the stubborn, impetuous woman. She'd been here less than twenty-four hours and had totally disrupted his life.

He looked up at the moon and smiled. So then why didn't he feel that bad about it?

FIVE

"It's not that I don't believe you," Kitty said to Elizabeth as she leaned her elbows on the tiled breakfast bar. "I'm not surprised you were acquainted with him. My dad made it his business to know everyone living here full-time, but church? Bible study? I can count the number of times he set foot in church on one hand. Not his favorite place."

"Really? How odd. He came to church and prayer meeting almost every week. He could be very—" Elizabeth smiled then finished "—opinionated. He obviously liked to push people's buttons and get a lively discussion going."

"Now *that* sounds like him. He had a gift for irritating people."

"I found him refreshing. He kept things from getting boring." She folded and stored the paper bags under the sink. "I miss him. I'm sorry for your loss. And I'm sorry for the loss to this town."

"Thank you." Kitty's eyes stung. "I'm afraid some people don't feel the way you do."

"Well *I* certainly don't believe any of those nasty rumors going around."

Kitty blinked hard. She wasn't going to cry, even if fatigue made her emotions ride close to the surface. She needed to focus on preserving her father's memory. "Did he attend prayer meeting the evening before the fire?"

"Yes, he did."

"Was he acting normally? I mean, did he seem agitated or worried?"

Elizabeth furrowed her brow. "The sheriff asked me the same question. Sam might've seemed a bit distracted, but other than that, everything seemed normal. You can ask Pastor James, Luke's father."

"So Luke wasn't at the meeting?"

"No, they were still in transition with the move and trying to renovate this place. James will have his own living space, yet still be close to Michael, when they are done. You should see Michael's attic bedroom. It's wonderful."

"Luke seems to be a multi-talented man. Where did he work before he came here?"

"They're originally from Chicago. James worked for a large church in downtown Chicago." Elizabeth turned and opened the refrigerator. "Are you hungry? I'll heat up the chicken rice soup I made last night."

"Sounds good," Kitty said, suddenly disgruntled. Obviously this woman was more than a causal friend. She seemed intricately involved in the Tanner household. "So Luke must've worked for the Chicago Fire Department, then?"

"Well...." She paused as the front door opened and shut.

Luke rounded the corner, carrying a large box and Kitty's duffel bag. "Sorry that took so long. The sheriff's team had to finish before I could retrieve your bag. Oh, hi, Elizabeth. I see you two have met."

"Yes we have," Elizabeth said. "I was telling her that James used to minister to a large congregation."

"Yep, he did for many years. I'm glad he has a chance to slow down now." Luke set the box and bag down. He brushed off the dust from his shirt and shifted his gaze to Kitty. "Your clothes were all over the floor. I hope I got them all. I also brought the box of your Dad's office things you wanted."

Kitty reached to open the lid.

"Maybe you should wait," Luke said. "I'll take it out on the deck and check for spiders first. A few black widows showed up in the garage."

She snatched back her hands with a shudder. "Good idea."

"Have you eaten, Luke?" Elizabeth asked. "I have leftover chicken soup on the stove. Your dad, Michael and I ate at Sarah's. James went back to the church to do some marriage counseling this evening, so I brought Michael home. Choir practice is in about forty minutes, but I can fix sandwiches before I go."

"Thanks, but we can manage, Elizabeth. I don't want to keep you," Luke said.

"Oh, it's no problem, I still have some time. You know how I love cooking for other people." Elizabeth smiled at him. "This afternoon I took the list off your refrigerator and got the groceries. James added some treats. He loves his shortbread cookies."

"Yes, he does, and I appreciate you picking up food." He glanced over his shoulder. "Where's Michael?"

Elizabeth sighed. "Where else? His room. He's in a horrible mood but won't say what happened at school. He wouldn't talk to his grandfather about it, either."

"Let me take this outside, and then I'll see if I can find out what the problem is." Luke lifted the box, and Kitty followed him onto the deck. He yanked the tape off the cardboard lid and spilled the contents out on the planking. "Wait a few minutes to let anything that wants to, crawl away."

"Fine with me." Kitty shivered as she eyed the heaps of paper, folders, and magazines.

Elizabeth sidled past Luke in the doorway and handed

Kitty a cold glass of lemonade. "It's such a nice evening, I'll bring supper out here." She gestured to a deck lounge. "Why don't you make yourself comfortable? The cushion's nice and soft."

"Thank you." Kitty eased her stiffening body into the chair, propped up her feet, and closed her eyes. Her tight muscles eased some, but her head ached. She rubbed her temples as she listened to the wind in the oaks.

"What's the matter with you? You have too much to drink?" a voice said near her ear.

Kitty jerked upward, eyelids snapping open to find Michael by her chair. She smothered a groan. "No, I don't drink alcohol, if that's what you mean. I hit my head today and it hurts."

"Why not?" The boy plopped down cross-legged on the deck, gazing intently at her.

"Why what? Why don't I drink?" she asked, and Michel nodded. "Because it's not allowed when I'm on duty, and besides, it's not good for me."

"Have you *ever* gotten drunk?"

Was he serious? Kitty shot a glance over her shoulder. Elizabeth moved about in the kitchen but Luke hadn't returned. No rescue in sight. She lowered her voice. "Okay, once, maybe twice, when I was young and stupid, but I don't anymore. It's not worth it."

"Did you throw up?"

"Yes, but that wasn't the worst part. We damaged school property and I got in big trouble." Actually it had been Evan in the driver's seat of the lawn tractor that tore through the hedge, knocked down the school sign and dented the PE teacher's car. Kitty, clinging to the seat back, had been too inebriated to realize Evan mowed out a dirty word on the football field before crashing to a stop. Her friend, sick to his stomach, conveniently stumbled away into the woods before the sheriff arrived.

"Did you go to jail?" Michael asked in an eager tone.

"Almost. My dad convinced the sheriff and principal to give me community service." She sighed. The sheriff would've loved to lock her up after the numerous stunts she and her friends had pulled, but he'd never had enough evidence against her. No one would snitch on each other either. In fact, she'd never turned Evan in for the vandalism. He still owed her. "I worked every day for a month after school picking up trash around the lake. It was pretty gross. Why do you want to know? Someone at school offer you a beer or something?"

Michael shrugged. "What happened to your head?"

"I hit a rock."

His eyes widened. "Cool. Is there blood? Can I see?"

Kitty sighed. "Not much, but you can look." She leaned forward and parted her hair. He gazed at her lump, and then sat back, seemingly disappointed at the lack of gore.

"Where'd you come from anyway? I thought your dad went upstairs to look for you."

"He did? Don't tell him I'm here." He scooted into the shadows, but a woof sounded behind them. Jack charged from the house, skidded to stop and rapidly sniffed Michael from head to bare toes.

Luke followed, a thunderous look on his face. "Michael Tanner, I told you never, ever to climb out your window unless it's an emergency. It disengages the alarm, but more importantly, what if you fell?"

Michael pushed the panting dog away. "I'm not that stupid."

"No, you're not. Which is why I'm grounding you from your PlayStation for the rest of the week."

Michael sprang to his feet. "That's not fair."

Luke shook his head. "What's *not* fair is that you know the rules and willfully broke them. Plus, you left your dog locked in your room. You know he's supposed to stay with you. Now go in and do your homework."

"I hate you!" Michael raced into the house, the dog bounding at his heels.

Luke let out a long sigh. "I'm sorry if he bothered you."

"Oh, it's fine, but we just had a strange conversation. He wanted to know if I was drunk. I know I look a bit battered but—"

Luke spun away, a strangled sound escaping his throat. He gripped the railing, and his back heaved with a deep breath.

"Are you okay?" Kitty asked, startled. "Did I say something wrong?"

Elizabeth strolled out onto the deck. "Dinner's ready. I hope you like homemade bread. I'm not the best baker in the world, but I can run a bread machine." She carried a tray holding a soup tureen, bowls and a crusty loaf and set it on the redwood picnic table. "We may not have many more mild nights like this. Already the leaves are changing color, which should bring up lots of tourists for the Fall Festival next week. My shop sure could use the business. Since the fire, sales have been down for everyone."

"It's hard to survive without the tourists," Kitty agreed, getting to her feet.

Elizabeth spied the pinecone. "Wow, look at that Coulter. I like to spray them gold and make Christmas decorations. They can be dangerous, though. Last winter one hit Franklin Davis's car and shattered the windshield."

Kitty glanced at Luke's inert profile silhouetted against the Four Sisters' gleaming snow caps. "I know what you mean. That one rolled off the roof and almost hit me. It left a dent in the deck."

"Where?" Luke asked, suddenly coming to life. He strode to where Kitty pointed to a scratch in the redwood plank and pulled a penlight from his pocket. After he examined the damage, he stepped back to shine the beam on the roof. "The trees around the house are oak. The nearest pine is about fifty feet away, and it's not a Coulter."

"Maybe Michael left it there during one of his adventures out his window." Elizabeth clapped a hand to her cheek. "I almost forgot. Kitty thought she heard someone on the roof earlier."

"But we didn't see anyone," Kitty added quickly as Luke's sharp gaze shifted to her. "Could've been the wind."

"I hope that's all it was," Elizabeth said, a tremor in her voice. "Now I've got to run. Mrs. Beasley gets agitated if we're late."

"I'll walk you to your car," Luke said.

Kitty followed them inside and waited by the stone fireplace until Luke returned. "I'm sorry."

"For which part of today?"

She stopped her restless pacing and grimaced. "Hey, you don't have to get sarcastic. I know I should've mentioned it the minute you came in, but I'm not sure if there actually was anyone on the roof."

"Did you also imagine the pinecone rolling off the roof at the precise moment you were under it?"

"No," she conceded as they stared at each for a couple beats. "Why would someone want to hurt me?"

"You tell me."

Kitty's eyes narrowed, anger slowly replacing the fear swirling through her. "You think this is my fault, don't you? That somehow this relates to my father."

"I don't know. That's the problem." He crossed his arms over his chest. "Let's start from the beginning. Someone allegedly called you in L.A., prompting you to come home.

Your father's cabin is ransacked twice. The station office is broken into. Someone tried to smash your head in with a shovel, and now, apparently with a pinecone. All within the space of twenty-four hours. Logically, this makes me wonder what *you're* hiding."

"Nothing." She held her hands out to her sides. "What you see is what you get, Chief Tanner."

"Okay, assuming that's true," he said, ignoring Kitty's retort, "let's examine this from a different angle. What did your father possess that someone is so anxious to get a hold of?"

The chill tickling her spine intensified. "I honestly don't know."

His gaze bore into hers for what seemed an eternity. "Stay there," he finally said, heading down the hall and bounding up the stairs to the attic bedroom. A minute ticked by, then the roof creaked. The hair on Kitty's arms stood up. She followed the sound to the front porch in time to see Luke's legs slip over the eave as he hung for a moment and then dropped to the railing. He caught his balance and looked at her.

She chewed on her lower lip and nodded. "Sounded the same."

He jumped to the porch. "Michael claims he never put the Coulter up there. There's only two easy ways to get up on the roof without a ladder—through the attic window or from the back deck railing. Both would mean access had to be through the house. The alarm was on all day, except for when you were here this afternoon. I'm going to secure every inch of this place. Tomorrow we're going to search your cabin and the station again. Then we'll retrace your father's steps before the fire."

"Okay," Kitty said, relieved he said "we." He wasn't cutting her out of the loop yet. Her gaze followed his to the road as a car rolled around the bend, its headlights flowing over a vehicle parked across the road. "Who brought my Jeep?"

"George Murphy. He's on duty tonight at the station." He handed the keys to her. "If you decide to drive around, let the sheriff and I know your destination."

Kitty pocketed the keys. "Is this akin to, 'please don't leave town or plan long trips'?"

"Hardly. I'd like nothing more than to see you go home, but while you're here, let's avoid any more hospital visits."

"I'll try to keep them to the minimum." Kitty trailed him to the dining room, trying to ignore the sting of his words. She wanted to go home too, but did he have to remind her of how unwelcome she was here?

Luke retrieved the tray of food, zapped the tureen in the microwave, then set it on the table. He ladled out two bowlfuls of soup. Kitty sipped the savory chicken broth, rich with brown rice and vegetables, and nibbled on the hearty bread, wonderfully flavored with a hint of molasses. If Elizabeth ever decided to trade in her craft store for a restaurant, she'd give Sarah a run for her money.

Kitty buttered another slice. Maybe she should invest in a bread machine. Her father never worried about her learning her way around a kitchen. She could handle the basics, but when she'd gotten engaged, Jordan insisted she take culinary lessons. "Every wife should know how to cook more than mac and cheese," he'd said. What if he wanted to bring fellow physicians or administrators home for dinner? Kitty grimaced, remembering her sharp reply on what he could do with his lessons. Had she been so unreasonable to resist being forced into a certain niche in his life? Why couldn't he love her for who she was?

"Are you doing okay?" Luke asked, settling in across the table.

"Just tired. The food is delicious. Your girlfriend is a wonderful cook."

Luke choked on his bread, and for a second Kitty thought she'd have to administer the Heimlich. "Elizabeth is just a friend."

"Really?" Kitty twirled her spoon, creating waves in her soup. "Does *she* know that?"

He coughed again. "When my dad moved here not long after my mom died, she and other church ladies took him under their wings. They fixed meals for him and helped him get settled. After Michael and I arrived, Elizabeth continued the habit out of the kindness of her heart."

"Okay, if you say so," Kitty said in a dubious tone.

Luke cocked his head. "I wouldn't have taken you for the jealous type."

"Excuse me?" Kitty snapped back against her chair. "What would I be jealous of? You're not even my type."

He paused with the spoon halfway to his mouth. "Okay. I'm curious. What kind of man do you prefer?"

Even though she assumed he was teasing, heat flooded from her toes to the roots of her hair. Minus a few of his annoying traits, like believing her father a murderer, Luke *might* be the type of guy she'd like to hang out with under different circumstances. "Actually, I'm not looking for any kind of romantic relationship. Been there, done that, and it ended badly."

"But if you were looking?"

Her pulse accelerated. "Aren't you getting a bit too personal, Chief Tanner? Is this your way of flirting?"

Luke grinned. "Didn't take you for the cowardly type, either. You seem like a decisive woman who goes after what she wants. Humor me—I'm looking for a distraction."

Humor him? Oh, what difference did it make? She blew

out a deep breath. "Okay, *if* I were looking for a boyfriend, he'd have to live near me in L.A."

"Ah, so geography disqualifies me." He continued to grin. "Guess I should be relieved. What other qualities would you deem necessary? Someone good-looking? Rich?"

She shook her head, a vision of Jordan and his Porsche floating through her mind. "Wealth and looks aren't important to me. I'd need someone kind and honest. Someone I can trust. Someone loyal. Someone...." Her heart squeezed painfully. Someone who loved her unconditionally.

He stared at her as the silence stretched. "Okay, this conversation has died a natural death. But if I were you, I'd be looking for someone proficient in first aid who can patch up your hard head."

She grimaced. "Very funny."

"Not even marginally, but it's the best I can do tonight." He stood and stacked the soiled dishes on the breakfast bar. "Color is back in your cheeks, so you must be feeling better."

"Wait a second. What would be your type of woman?"

He paused for so long, she thought he hadn't heard her. "Someone good for Michael," he finally said, returning to the table. "Ready to work?"

"Let's get it done," Kitty said, glad for some action to distract her from the disturbing emotions the conversation had unearthed. Jordan had wanted children right away, another reason he thought her job unsuitable.

She forced herself to concentrate on sorting the material into piles as Luke brought in armloads from the deck. Magazines covered with sticky notes marking equipment her dad had wanted, various newspaper articles and a yellow legal pad filled with drafts of letters and memos.

Luke blew the dust off a *Mountain Living* magazine. "As I mentioned, we already went through everything, but maybe you can recognize something odd." He rifled through a newspaper stack. "Like, why did he keep all these clippings?"

Kitty shrugged, gazing at the mess with affection. "Dad was a closet pack rat. He kept everything well organized at work, but he'd squirrel away stuff like this. He especially liked keeping anything related to the fire department. He'd started several scrapbooks on the department's history. They should be at the station."

"Haven't seen them. I'll take another look tomorrow."

Kitty glanced up and drew in a sharp breath. "Where'd you get that notebook?"

"From my pocket." He held up the small, spiral-bound pad that he'd been making a note in.

"No, I meant, did you get it from the station?"

"Nope. Picked it up at the store. Why?

Kitty slumped back in her chair. "My dad used to carry similar notebooks to keep to-do lists, notes to add to his reports and other stuff he wanted to remember. He never threw them away in case he needed to refer back to something."

Luke frowned and rubbed his chin. "To my knowledge, no such notebooks were found, or the sheriff would've confiscated them. Maybe they're still in the cabin."

"I looked briefly this morning, but he used to store them at the station." She sighed wearily. It'd take days to search through everything, especially now since someone trashed both the office and cabin.

From the front of the house came the sound of a door creaking open, followed by a rhythmic thumping. "We're in here, Dad," Luke called.

An elderly gentleman using a cane limped around the corner. "Well, well, well, this must be the Miss McGuire I've heard so much about today. I'm Luke's father, James Tanner."

Kitty smiled. "You must frequent Sarah's Café too."

"Best place to eat in town and to hear the local news."

She shook his proffered hand. "That's what my dad used to say, only he called it gossip."

"Ah, yes, Sam." James squeezed her fingers before releasing them. "He played a mean chess game. Beat me almost every time. You probably don't recall, considering the circumstances, but you and I met at the funeral."

Under the glow of the hanging lamp, Kitty studied the kind, deeply lined face. He seemed familiar, and not just because he resembled Luke. A few inches shorter than his son, James sported the same full head of hair—but his was streaked with silver—and lively eyes, dark as coal. He leaned on his shiny wooden cane, his shoulders slightly hunched, as if bowed from a lifetime carrying other people's burdens. "Oh, I remember now. You offered a prayer at the graveside. I appreciated the insightful, kind things you said."

"You're welcome—I meant every word." His smile sent warmth rushing through her.

"There's soup and bread if you're hungry." Luke looked up from an ear-marked supply catalog.

"Tempting. I do love Elizabeth's soup, but Sarah fed me well, *much* too well." James patted his stomach. "Besides, it's getting late. Early to bed, early to rise guarantees good fishing in the morning, in the lake and for the two-legged kind." He chuckled. "Does Michael need help with his homework? We didn't get a chance to do it this afternoon."

"I don't know. He's upset and not talking to me," Luke said. "He had his books out when I was in his room earlier."

"I'll check on him." James smiled at Kitty again. "I hope we get a chance to get acquainted. Your father said many wonderful things about you."

He did? Kitty blinked in surprise. "I—I would like that. Thank you."

"Kitty's going to be our houseguest tonight. Someone

broke into Sam's cabin again." Luke briefly recapped the day's events for his father's benefit.

"Troubling things have been stirring in this town lately." James said, shaking his head. "Makes me feel like I'm not doing my job well enough. Maybe I need to double my prayers." He winked at Kitty. "Well, grandson duty calls. I'll see you at breakfast. Welcome to our home, Miss McGuire."

"Thank you, and please call me Kitty."

"Only if you call me James. 'Night all." He ambled down the hall.

"You and your dad seem close." Kitty said.

"I guess as close as most." Luke lifted a wrinkled, yellow bill of sale up to the light.

"Were you always?" she asked, hating the wistful edge to her voice.

"There were times he didn't approve of my lifestyle, so I didn't visit as often as I should've. I regret that now, especially since Mom died a few years back."

Interesting. She and Tanner had something in common. Only he'd been given time to correct the situation, and now she couldn't. "I'm sorry about your mom."

"Thanks. Dad misses her more, of course. They genuinely enjoyed each other. Right now he seems content working part-time and helping with Michael. His support, and the church members' prayers, got us through a really rough period."

"You're lucky," she said, although she considered herself more of an action-taker than someone who prayed. Sure, she talked to God on occasion, but didn't feel a need to belong to a church where busybodies looked for opportunities to criticize. She nibbled on her lower lip. Had her dad ever prayed for her? With his new interest in religion, she supposed anything was possible.

"Is your head bothering you? You're pale again. Maybe you should lie down."

"I just want to get through this pile, and then I'll turn in." She sorted through the newspaper clippings. Some were articles and pictures of various fires around Pine Valley. Others featured auto accidents where the fire department used the Jaws of Life to free the victims from mangled steel prisons.

She paused over the photo of her father receiving a plaque for Citizen of the Year. She'd been so proud of him, but instead of celebrating with her, he'd gone out with his buddies. She threw the clipping down and stood. "I think I'll take a shower if that's okay."

Luke looked up from his growing stack of invoices. "Guest room is second door on the right before you get to the new addition. Bathroom is across the hall. The plumbing isn't finished for the new apartment, so we have to share the one shower. Lock the door to ensure privacy. Extra towels are in the cabinet."

"Thanks." Kitty hoisted her duffel bag and trudged to her assigned room. Glass lined the outside wall, and a sliding door opened to the deck. The décor, a simple southwestern design of soft peaches and greens, exuded a peaceful atmosphere with soothing scents of pine and cedar. She looked forward to burying herself under the down comforter for a few blissful hours of oblivion.

She unzipped her bag and chose blue sweats to wear to bed. As Kitty lifted her cosmetic bag, a wrinkled piece of paper fluttered out. She held it under the nightstand lamp and could barely decipher the smeared typed words.

So that they shall take no wood—
any out of the forests,

they shall burn the weapons
and rob them that robbeth them s—
Eze

The jagged edge indicated someone had ripped the sheet. She dumped out the bag's contents but couldn't find the missing half. Strange. The note must've been in her dad's cabin and gotten mixed up in her scattered clothing. She turned the paper over, and her stomach clenched. The handwritten words "Transgressions of man shall" slashed darkly across the page in her father's handwriting, and underneath were the Roman numerals *VI III*.

They shall burn the weapons? Luke hadn't mentioned seeing this or the rest of the note. It could be something her father jotted down from church, but for someone suspected of arson and murder, this note might seem highly incriminating. Even with their apparent cooperation, she still couldn't trust Luke or the sheriff to be objective. They were searching for a scapegoat.

Of course, she'd have to turn the note over soon or be accused of withholding evidence. But, if possible, she needed to find the missing half first. A few hours or days wouldn't make any difference in the ongoing investigation. She stuffed the paper deep into her bag and limped to the shower.

The hot water soothed her muscle aches, and she wasn't as stiff when she slipped into her worn, comfortable sweats and tank top. She returned to her room, clicked off the lamp and slid between the silky-smooth sheets. Laying on her side, she gazed at the stars floating high above the Four Sisters.

She still found it hard to believe her father had flip-flopped his beliefs and joined the church. He'd been so adamant they didn't need the pious, insincere charity some of the congregation offered. He didn't need more people to tell him he wasn't living his life well enough. Hadn't his ex-wife and her wayward mother done a great job with that? The memory of her parents arguing sent heartache searing through her chest.

No matter what happened, she needed to concentrate on the present and protecting Nana's state of mind. She'd make sure Sam McGuire would always be a hero in his mother's eyes.

Kitty padded over to her jeans and retrieved her cell phone. She speed-dialed the nursing home where the nurse informed her Netty McGuire had retired for the evening, and unless it was an emergency to please call back in the morning. Lonely granddaughter didn't constitute an emergency. She returned to bed and counted backward from a thousand. Sleep finally drifted close when a knock startled her.

"Come in." Kitty sat up, her pulse quickening as Luke crossed the room to the sliding door and picked up two thin steel rods.

"The wired security system covers the front and back doors and window, but if you want to let the air in at night, keep the shorter rod in place. Use the longer one for when it's closed. Normally I don't worry about the deck because no one can access it except—"

"—from the roof."

Luke nodded. "Exactly, so we'll take extra precautions. Also, Jack's allowed to roam the house at night, so if you get up, try not to surprise him. Whistle or talk so he knows you're there."

"Okay," Kitty said, deciding she'd stay in bed till dawn.

Luke returned to the hallway. "Don't be alarmed if Dad or I check on you in a couple hours. Doctor's orders."

She groaned. "Do I have a choice?"

"Nope. I'll leave your door open a bit. Call me if you need anything." His footsteps faded, and then the stairs creaked.

"Goodnight to you, too," she said to the empty room,

wide-awake again. Her shoulder began to ache from where she'd hit the ground. She tossed and turned, trying to get more comfortable. After a few minutes voices drifted from the floor above, then just one droned on and on. Luke must be reading to Michael. Who knew if a child Michael's age appreciated it, but she gave Luke points for effort. She'd have loved it if her father had read to her.

She snuggled under the puffy quilt. Although she couldn't make out the words, the murmur of Luke's voice was surprisingly reassuring. He may be stubborn, opinionated and bossy, but he tried to be a good man and father. She sighed and her eyes closed. No, she wouldn't mind having him check up on her after all.

SIX

Kitty bolted upright in bed, gasping for air. Her limbs ached, muscles cramping, as if she perched high on the rocky face of the Four Sisters trying to find her father. One false move would bring certain death. It had only been a bad dream, but terror still swirled thickly.

She fumbled for the lamp beside her bed and squeezed her eyes shut against the explosion of light. A weak scent of smoke hovered in the air. The fire station siren wailed in the distance. She struggled to wrestle free of the tangled sheets clinging to her damp body. The door suddenly burst open and she stifled a scream. Michael, clad in red Spiderman pajamas, stood in the doorway. Jack peered around his knees, ears back and eyes wary.

"Don't you know how to knock? You scared me." Kitty kicked off the covers, but a throbbing behind her ear kept her from leaping up. She slid her legs over the mattress edge. "Where's your father?"

"He's gone to the station. He said you could take me with you."

"No offense, but I'm not your babysitter." She scanned the floor for boots.

"I'm not a baby. I'm almost eleven. And other kids get to watch."

She discovered the missing boot under the bed and yanked it out. "Then why didn't he take you?"

"He doesn't trust me." He said the words with such bitterness, Kitty paused to stare at him. He fisted his hands at his side, his stance defiant and angry, but tears glistened in his dark eyes. "He thinks I need to be watched every second. That's why you need to be with me."

Michael darted past her, lifted the safety rod and pushed the door open. "Come on, I can see the fire!"

Kitty dropped her boots and ran to the dark deck with Jack. The crisp air and cold planking under her bare feet whisked away any remaining sleep cobwebs. Michael perched on the railing, his legs dangled out into space.

"Michael, get off of there!" She snagged the back of Michael's pajama top. "Do you want to break your neck?"

Michael shot her a disdainful look. "I'm not going to fall," he said, but to her relief he swung his legs over and hopped down. "Look." He pointed below to where flames shot above the tree line near her cabin.

Kitty dashed into the bedroom as the station siren abruptly stopped, replaced by the softer wails of the fire engines. She snatched up her jeans and raced to the bathroom. When she emerged, Michael stood in the living room, also dressed in jeans and shoes.

"I'm ready."

She shook her head. "If your father won't take you, I certainly can't."

"But he *said* it was okay, and you can't leave me here all alone."

She patted her pockets for her keys and headed for the front door. "You're not alone. Your grandfather is here."

"No he's not! Check for yourself." He pointed at the intercom.

She paused. Was he telling the truth? She hustled over

to the intercom and pressed the button. "Hello, James?" No reply. She looked at Michael. "How does this thing work?"

"Like this." He punched the same button and called his grandfather. Still no response. "See? I told you. He went to the hospital to see a sick person."

Kitty bit her lower lip. If someone had summoned the pastor this late, it had to be an emergency. But he or Luke should've communicated with her before leaving her in charge of a child she barely knew. She couldn't leave the boy here, even if he had a dog with huge fangs to protect him. She hurried down the hall to double-check and tried the door to the addition. Locked. She knocked and when no one answered, she turned to Michael.

"Call your father on his cell. Now."

Michael punched the speed dial on the portable phone and handed the receiver to her. The connection went directly to Luke's voice mail. "Hey Tanner, I'm heading down the hill. No one is here to stay with Michael so I'm bringing him with me. I'll make sure he stays safe. See you in a few minutes."

She tossed the phone on the couch. "Okay, let's do this. Can you behave?"

He rolled his eyes. "Can you?"

"You can start by being respectful to your elders," she said as he deactivated the alarm and opened the front door. She groaned inwardly. She'd been in charge of Michael for less than fifteen minutes and already she sounded as bossy as her father had been.

Jack shoved his way between them. "Will he obey?" Kitty asked.

"Jack, heel," Michael said with another eye roll. The dog snapped to attention beside him.

Apprehension swelled in her chest as she scanned the dark road for any sign of movement. "Listen to me—you must promise to do exactly what I say and stay out of trouble."

"Whatever." He skipped toward the steps.

Kitty grabbed Michael's arm and Jack's growled. "What was that?"

"Okay, okay, I promise." He jerked from her grasp and sprinted to the Jeep. Kitty followed, shaking her head. Anxiety overrode her common sense, but her gut screamed at her to get to the fire as fast as possible.

Kitty unlocked the doors. Jack jumped in and scrambled on top of a bundle on the back seat. "Don't let him sit on the fire shelters. If they get torn, they're useless."

Michael pulled the dog to the floor and they sped forward, gravel spewing behind the tires. She clenched her teeth as they tore down the road, and rounded the last bend. As she'd feared, the call hadn't been for a wildlands fire. Flames engulfed her father's cabin. Her cabin.

Home.

She slammed on the brakes. The Jeep slid to a stop, and she leapt out, towing Michael by the sleeve to one of the parked fire engines. She hoisted him into the cab and patted the seat until the dog jumped in beside him. "Wait right here and keep Jack with you."

Even at this safe distance heat engulfed them, bringing tears to her eyes. She waved at George Murphy the engineer, busy with the controls on the engine's pump, and motioned to Michael sitting in the cab. His mouth fell open at the sight of her, but then he grinned and gave her a thumbs up.

Flames flashed along the top third of the cabin walls and under the eaves despite the water streaming on three sides. She paced along the perimeter of the action zone, yearning to help, even though she knew they were doing everything possible. Unless she went back to the station, she didn't have the protective gear to allow her any closer.

Near the base of the facing wall, something long and white wiggled. She inched closer to get a better look. Someone had covered the opening to the crawl space beneath the cabin. A spindly, fur-covered leg poked out between two logs piled against the concrete block.

Max!

The cat clawed desperately, trying to free himself. If the house collapsed, he'd be crushed. No one was in earshot to hear her call for help. She glanced back at the wall. If she hurried, she could kick away the logs and be back to the safety zone in a seconds. Ducking low into the cooler air, she raced forward. She'd almost reached the logs when something knocked her sideways. Gloved hands clamped down on her arms, lifting her. Luke's steely arms engulfed her, his body blocking her from the worst of the heat.

"Are you crazy? You can't go in," he yelled, his voice muffled by the face shield.

"I know!" Kitty pushed ineffectively against his yellow jacket. His hold tightened. "Let me go. Max is under there."

Ash, like dirty snowflakes, landed on his helmet. He shook his head as if he didn't understand and hoisted her off her feet, walking her backward toward the engines. She futilely kicked at his shins covered in thick turnout gear. "Put me down! He'll die," she yelled, but he continued to carry her until they were beside the engine. He plopped her on her feet.

He lifted his shield. "Are you trying to get killed? You can't go in there without protective gear."

"I wasn't trying to get inside. Max is under the house."

"Max?"

"My cat! He's trapped. I need to move those logs." She pointed to where the white leg reappeared. "Look! There he is. You can't let him die like that." A window exploded, glass and sparks showered down. "Please!"

"Stay here—I'll get him." He motioned to a group of men

armed with hoses. Two firefighters moved sideways as a unit until the stream hit the roof above the crawl space. Luke ran through the billowing steam and kicked the logs aside. A flash of white streaked past him and bounded into the woods.

Kitty sagged against the fire engine as Luke jogged back to her. He lifted his shield, wiping his gloved hand over his glistening face. "Did he get out?"

"Yes!" She impulsively threw her arms around him. The buckles on his coat dug into her cheek, but she didn't care.

He awkwardly patted her back. "Hey, it's all right. It's only a building. The cat's safe."

She nodded but clung harder, craving the security of his arms while her former world crumbled. He hesitated for a moment and then pulled her closer, holding her tightly until her knees stopped trembling. "You're going to be okay." His breath warmed her ear. "We'll get through this."

She lifted her head. Their gazes locked. Understanding softened his usually tense features. The painful knot of emotions eased in her chest and hope flickered to life. Oh, how she wanted to trust this man. To not feel so alone. To forget the past and care about somebody with all her heart. Could she dare try again?

His gaze shifted over her head and his body tensed. "What's Michael doing here?"

She glanced over her shoulder at the boy in the cab. "I brought him."

"What?" he thundered, sending a jolt through Kitty as if she'd been doused with ice water. "How dare you take my son out of the house without my permission."

"Hey! What was I supposed to do? I couldn't leave him there alone."

"What do you mean alone? Where's my father?"

"I don't know. Michael said he went to the hospital to see someone."

Luke shook his head. "He wouldn't go without telling me."

"Chief," a firefighter yelled from the front line.

"Stay here. Watch Michael and stay out of trouble."

Kitty nodded, stunned by his cold, harsh tone. Only moments before she'd thought there had been a bond growing between them. Just went to prove she was still a poor judge of people. Like father, like daughter. He'd trusted a woman who'd betrayed him, and she'd given her love to Jordan who'd stomped on it when things didn't go his way.

She ran her palms over her heat-stung face. Luke was under stress and overreacting. Obviously there was some confusion, but she'd tried to contact James, and she hadn't put Michael in harm's way.

She leaned against the engine's bumper and watched Luke on the perimeter of the danger zone. Fog engulfed the cabin and the nearby trees. A firefighter heaved an ax at the large bay window her father had proudly installed. Part of her heart shattered as the glass exploded.

Kitty knew from experience the structure was doomed. The firefighters' next course of action would be to prevent the fire from spreading to the forest. Logically, she realized the building could be replaced. No one had died. Not even Max. But logic didn't stop the pieces of her childhood from dying as, one by one, interior walls collapsed with roars of splintering wood. The roof caved in with a deafening crash that echoed against the steep mountain range and sent sparks toward the heavens.

Kitty sank to the damp ground and wrapped her arms around her knees. "It's just a house. Just wood and nails," she murmured. Oh, who was she kidding? This place mattered to her, just like every home mattered to countless other victims of structure fires. She hadn't felt this powerless since the day her mother abandoned her, or as alone as when she'd stood over her father's fresh grave.

A standing exterior wall swayed. Another firefighter, dangerously close to the cabin, directed a stream of water through a window. Above his head, the logs shifted and bent in the heat. Kitty bolted forward, waving her arms, her voice swallowed in the bellow of crumbling wood.

Luke charged past her, tackled the firefighter and rolled them away from the falling timber. Kitty followed, kicking the glowing embers off their coats and pants. The discarded hose pulled loose from under the fallen beams and writhed like a giant snake, whipping the deadly brass nozzle through the air.

"Watch out!" Luke yelled as the nozzle swung toward her. She dropped to the ground and covered her head with her arms. A direct hit from the flying metal could kill. The hose flipped over her and began to recoil. When the nozzle hit the ground, she threw herself on the bucking hose as the engineer cut the water pressure.

She lay for a moment catching her breath, and then crawled to where Luke dragged the fallen firefighter. He shook the man's shoulder. "Are you okay?"

The helmet bobbed up and down. He shook off Luke's grip and got to his feet.

"Good, then you can walk home and stay there. You're on suspension." Luke threw up his hands in a disgusted gesture and marched off toward the engine.

"B-but why?" a young voice shouted from behind the face shield.

Kitty groaned as Luke spun around. She eased out of the line of fire.

"Why? You have to ask why? What did you think you were doing?" Luke barked. "You know better than to stand next to a collapsing structure. You could've been killed. And there should've been two men tending that hose."

The firefighter hung his head. "Sorry, Chief. I guess I wasn't thinking."

"You're right you weren't thinking. You're on suspension until you get some sense in that hard head of yours." Luke turned and spied Kitty in the shadows. "And you…!" He threw up his hands in a futile gesture and stomped away.

"You're welcome," she shouted after him and gingerly touched her sore ribs where she'd fallen on the nozzle. She brushed off her clothes and stood awkwardly with the chastised firefighter. She couldn't blame Luke for being shaken, but did he have to be so harsh? The guys up here were volunteers.

"He'll probably change his mind when he calms down." Cool air bathed her face, and a faint scent of singed hair, probably her own, tickled her nose.

The man pulled off his helmet and grinned, his white teeth gleaming above his sooty chin. "Don't worry about it. I'm always on suspension until they need me."

Kitty gasped. "Jeremy Wright! What are you doing here? I thought you'd moved to Tahoe after high school."

"Didn't work out. I came home to help run Pop's sporting goods store." His gaze darted over her head. "Sorry about your dad's cabin. Glad you weren't in it. These old places go up too quick for us to do much."

Kitty nodded, a lump forming in her throat. "You guys did the best you could."

"Want some coffee? I grabbed a thermos from the station." He opened the cab door and Jack growled. "Whoa. Watch out." He backed away. "Hey, Michael, reach under the seat and get the big thermos and the cups."

"Can I have coffee?" Michael asked, tossing the items to Jeremy.

"Sure. I'm cool with it." Jeremy cranked off the lid and poured hot, steaming liquid into a cup. "Figure I can't get into any worse trouble."

Kitty intercepted the cup. "Better ask your dad, Michael."

From the kid's scowl, she surmised it wouldn't be okay with Luke. "I'll get you some bottled water from my car."

"Just a second," Jeremy rounded the truck's rear, and after he returned, he tossed a soda bottle to Michael. "Murphy's secret stash."

"Thanks." Kitty said, gratefully sipping the strong brew and studying the man leaning against the bumper. Jeremy trailed two grades behind her and was such a frequent visitor in the principal's office they'd given him his own chair. Time hadn't dimmed the mischievous gleam in his eye or tamed the rust-colored tangles falling over his forehead. The extra padding from the thick, yellow turnout gear expanded his thin frame, making him appear strong and capable. Her dad started training him for firefighting at the age of sixteen. At least her father had believed Jeremy would turn out okay, even if most townspeople harbored doubts.

"How's your family?" Kitty asked, determined to ignore the cracking and popping noises behind her.

Jeremy shrugged. "Okay, although Pop and I bang heads in the store. He's not interested in any of my ideas. Won't even consider putting in a bigger snowboard stock. The man hasn't been out on the slopes in fifteen years."

Kitty gave him an empathetic smile. "Some people find change difficult."

He sighed. "Sometimes I think we would've been better off if the store had burned in the Wildcat fire. At least we'd have the insurance money to start over. It's like we're in the dark ages. I know they pay us to be on duty and stuff, but it's not the same as having professionally trained personnel. When I came back from Tahoe, I petitioned for some funding to take classes in Sacramento, and the Council turned me down flat, the idiots." His eyes sparked with anger. "Now after the last firestorm, they're *finally* considering putting out the funds to pay for more full-time firefighters. They vote on it next month. I plan on being the first they send for training."

Kitty pressed her lips together. Not if Luke kept suspending Jeremy.

"Tanner won't last," Jeremy said, sensing her thought. He gazed at Luke, who'd taken a turn on a hose, spraying nearby pines.

"Why do you say that?" Kitty asked, irked by his smug tone.

"He doesn't seem to like the job—and he spends a lot of time with Sheriff Johnson. Daniel's the incident commander most of the time. I'm surprised he's not here tonight."

"Tanner must have lots of experience for a newcomer to be hired so quickly. You'd think Daniel or Murphy would've been in line for the fire chief."

"Apparently the executive committee made the decision. Sarah was fit to be tied with Daniel getting passed over. She stormed into the mayor's office and gave him what for." Jeremy grinned. "I'd loved to have been there."

He pushed a button on his watch. "After three already...I better go. I have to open the store in the morning." He gave her a brief hug. "Be careful, okay?" He shot a dark, meaningful glance at Luke as he strode past.

After Jeremy slipped away into the shadows, she crawled into the engine cab beside Michael. Kitty leaned her head back against the seat, comforted by the vibrating roar of the pump engine behind her. Firefighting was her world, her reality, even as the past went up in smoke.

Two of her oldest friends, Evan and now Jeremy, had warned her about Luke. Yet despite their earlier argument, her intuition still whispered that he was a decent, honorable man. She just hoped her intuition wasn't wrong. She needed him.

Dawn broke with a pink glow over the mountain range. A forest service truck arrived on scene and dispatched a team of three to watch for spot fires. Kitty climbed from the engine cab so Murphy could resume his position behind the wheel. For the last four hours, she'd waited alone, watching her home turn to cinder and ash. James Tanner had collected his grandson around four in the morning. Michael protested all the way to the car.

Luke motioned they were leaving. After another fruitless search for Max, she retrieved her Jeep and followed his Bronco back to the Tanner home. Luke hadn't said another word to her since the incident with Jeremy, for which Kitty was grateful. Her nerves were stretched so painfully thin, if he even looked at her wrong, she'd snap. Judging from the taut muscles in Luke's face, he felt the same way. He opened the front door for her and then strode down the hall and up the stairs to the attic bedroom.

The smell of frying onions hung heavy in the air, causing Kitty to detour into the dining room. James lounged at the table with a newspaper fanned out in front of him. His balding head gleamed in the streaming sunlight.

"Ah, ha, the other runaway has returned," he said in a stern voice, but the crinkles around his eyes deepened as he smiled. "Everything under control down there?"

Kitty nodded. "Luckily, there was no wind, and the fire didn't spread to the forest."

James peered at her over his reading glasses. "We can thank God for that."

Kitty smothered a negative retort. Why should she thank God when He'd let her home burn to the ground?

"Everything happens for a reason," James added intuitively.

"If there is anything I can do to make this easier for you, let me know."

"Thanks, but I'll be fine," she said over the rising lump in her throat. She came from tough McGuire stock. Her father wouldn't cry over a burned structure.

"Help yourself to coffee. Breakfast is almost ready," Elizabeth called from her position at the stove frying eggs and hash browns.

Kitty poured herself a mug of coffee, not really surprised to see the other woman. Despite what Luke said about Elizabeth being only a friend, she obviously worked hard on making herself indispensable in the Tanner household.

"I'm sorry we alarmed you last night, James," Kitty said, cradling the warm mug in her chilled hands. "We tried to call you on the intercom. Michael said you'd left for the hospital."

"Yes, the boy has quite the imagination when he wants something. Too bad he doesn't apply that creative streak in school." James limped over to the intercom and examined the box. "See, here's the problem. The wire is unplugged in the back. Now, who do you suppose did that?"

"Michael. He tricked me," Kitty said, feeling even more stupid at being duped since this stunt might have been something she'd pull as a kid.

"No wonder it was so quiet. I should've known something was up." James maneuvered the wire back into place. "Should work fine now. Luke asked me last night to check on you every couple hours. I left the door to my side of the house open just in case you needed something. These walls are built really solid and my hearing isn't what it used to be."

"Michael must've locked your door. I knocked," she said. "I'll know better next time." Not that there would *ever* be a next time. She felt quite certain Luke would never leave her alone with his son again. "I'm sorry for the trouble I caused."

"Michael lied, and if anyone is to blame, it's me for being a lousy parent," Luke said as he came down the hall. "I've already grounded him. He knows the rules but chose to disobey them."

"If you're a lousy parent, what does that make me? I didn't even realize you all were gone." James said. "You're too hard on yourself and have a very short memory. Michael's smart and takes after you in many ways. Good and bad."

Kitty turned to Luke. "I'm not excusing his behavior, but he really wanted to be on scene with you. Maybe you should take him with you sometimes when it's safe. Involve him in your work." She narrowed her gaze. "Besides, if you hadn't gone off and left me, this wouldn't have happened."

"I didn't wake you because you should've stayed in bed."

"That wasn't an option. If the situation were reversed, what would you have done?"

"Breakfast's ready," Elizabeth called, bustling out of the kitchen. "Come get it while it's hot."

"We'll talk later," Luke said to Kitty, leading the way to the dining area,

"You're an angel, Elizabeth Greene," James said, removing his newspaper from the table, and helping her with the platters of scrambled eggs sprinkled with shredded cheese and crusty hash browns.

She smiled at James, her cheeks as pink as the floral blouse she wore. "It's the least I can do. I'm so grateful for our firefighters and those who support them. I could make pancakes, too, if anyone wants them."

"This looks mighty fine to me." James took a pitcher of orange juice from Elizabeth. "I suppose I could survive on my own cooking. And maybe with Luke's." He shot a grin at his son, who was moving the piles of Sam's papers to the floor. "But I'm happy to let someone else do it."

"Anytime...anywhere." Elizabeth patted James on the shoulder.

Kitty excused herself to go wash the black grime from her hands. Had it only been a few hours since she showered? She peered in the bathroom mirror. Heat-singed strands curled around her ash-covered cheeks. Soot streaked her shirt and jeans, but at least she wasn't bleeding anywhere this time. She returned to the dining room to hear Luke recounting Jeremy's near miss with the wall.

"I don't know why you keep him on the department," Elizabeth said, untying her apron and hanging it on a hook. "He's going to get himself or someone else killed."

Kitty settled into an empty chair and helped herself to a slice of hearty toast. "Oh, Jeremy's a good guy. Everyone makes mistakes. My dad thought he had a lot of potential."

"He does have enthusiasm," James said with a small smile.

"Is that what you call it?" Luke snorted. "Well, his 'enthusiasm' smashed an engine into a tree last month. Tore the bumper off. This was after he over-pressurized some air tanks, and one of them blew its top in the middle of a drill." He scooped more hash browns onto his plate and passed the platter to Kitty, addressing her directly. "He's accident-prone. Trouble follows him, and it'd be wise for you to avoid him."

Kitty set down the platter with a clank. "I appreciate your concern, but Jeremy and I are old friends."

"Jeremy could use more friends," James said. "He's either off by himself, or hanging with the party crowd. I've been trying to get him to join the young adult class at church."

"I'll encourage him too." Elizabeth picked up a tooled-leather handbag off one of the chairs. "I have to go open the shop. Call me if you need anything."

James pushed back his chair. "Thank you for the breakfast, Elizabeth, and if the rest of you will excuse me, I need to get to the library to finish my research for tonight's prayer meeting." He turned to Luke. "Unless you want me to stick around until Michael wakes up."

Luke shook his head. "Thanks, but I called the school and told them I'd drop him off at noon."

Kitty shoveled in the rest of her breakfast and gathered plates to take to the kitchen.

"You don't have to clean up after us," Luke said following her into the kitchen.

"I want to help. I don't feel right imposing on your hospitality, especially after last night. I didn't mean to cause trouble for Michael."

"Michael creates his own trouble," Luke said on a sigh. He flipped the dishwasher door shut. "The dishes can wait."

Kitty turned to him. "Any clue what started the fire?" she asked anxiously.

"Judging from how fast the place went up, I think an accelerant was used, but we'll know more after the county investigator gets up here." He placed a hand on her shoulder, guiding her to the living room. "I'm sorry. If this was arson, we'll catch whoever did it."

The edge of pity in his voice caused her to stiffen. "You bet we will. Meanwhile, it looks like the council and I'll just have to haggle over the insurance money," she quipped, but the words fell flat. "I want to get back to work. Can we head to Wildcat Ravine today?"

"Let's grab a couple of hours sleep first." He gazed at her with a worried expression. "You sure you're up for that?"

"No, but it's something I *have* to do."

SEVEN

Luke slicked back his wet hair and groaned at his reflection in the foggy mirror. Stress and fatigue had deepened wrinkles around his eyes and the dingy pallor of his skin. What a nightmare the last six hours had been. Kitty nearly gave him a coronary when she'd raced toward the burning structure like a crazy woman, risking her life for a cat. Then Jeremy…he didn't even want to think about his close call with the crumbling wall.

To make matters worse, Michael lied his way on scene. The child's deceit would have to be dealt with, but maybe Kitty was right. Maybe he should let Michael occasionally observe him at the fire station. Maybe it would bring them closer together. He seemed much more excited about firefighting than carpentry.

Luke shuddered, remembering the wall that had nearly collapsed on Jeremy. Was he insane? He'd have to think long and hard about taking Michael anywhere even remotely dangerous. The cutting memory of nearly losing Michael hovered too fresh. He'd learned the hard way that anything can happen in a matter of seconds and change your life forever. Latent terror surged through him.

Oh, Lord, what am I going to do? Michael's lies are becoming more frequent, and he rebels against the simplest rules. Thank You for protecting him last night, but please guide me on how to handle the child before something horrible happens to him. Again.

The constant anxiety he felt for his son abated some, but anger lingered. In the past, his work at the Bureau had never collided with his personal life until Michael's kidnapping. Luke had spent nine months of torture, self-recrimination and promises to God and himself that if he ever recovered Michael, he'd never let down his guard. Yet… he'd allowed a stranger into their home.

A target.

First chance he got, he'd tell the sheriff they had to make other arrangements for Miss McGuire, preferably convincing her to return home. Much as he liked the feisty woman, he couldn't risk putting Michael in danger. Surely she'd understand.

Decision made, he hung up his damp towel and, taking a deep breath, crossed the hall to the guest room. He knocked on the door, and it swung slowly open. Atop the bed, Kitty lay asleep on her side, still clutching a newspaper clipping. Other sheets of paper were scattered about the mattress. Her slender back rose and fell gently with each breath. Tangled curls covered her face.

"Kitty?" He moved closer. Her hair smelled like burnt wild flowers. He brushed the locks away from her eyes. The bruise from the attack at Fish Creek Camp had deepened to a dark purple. She moaned and puckered her eyebrows as if in pain. A wave of tenderness flowed through Luke, startling him. His whole life had been about defending those who couldn't protect themselves, and whether he liked it or not, this woman needed his help.

Lord, why me? Why now?

He rocked back on his heels and stuffed his hands in his

back pockets. She slept deeply, almost too deeply. Surely, she was out of danger from her head injury by now, but….

He covered her with an extra quilt and fought the strong urge to kiss her on the forehead.

Focus on the job, Tanner!

He exhaled sharply and tugged the clipping from her hand. Grabbing the rocking chair from the corner, he shoved it into the hall. Better safe than sorry. He'd be positioned between Kitty and Michael in case either one of them needed him. He slouched in the wooden frame, his tired muscles protesting.

He yawned. He needed sleep but his mind raced, poring over the details of the fire. Old cabins burning down wasn't unusual. Dry rotted wood, faulty wiring, lightning strikes, leaky gas lines—there were numerous explanations. But with the rapid flare-up at Kitty's cabin, he surmised someone used accelerant. The county fire investigator was already coming up to retrieve the canister they'd found at the campground, and now he also could examine the cabin site. Luke's gut told him the two incidents were related.

His hand still held the newspaper clipping Kitty had been studying. He examined the cramped notes penciled in the news column. Sam's handwriting, very familiar to him now, could sometimes be difficult to decipher. In this case, he'd simply made a note about a sprinkler system for the new hotel. Obviously, the system hadn't been completed before the Wildcat fire reduced the new construction to ashes.

He yawned again and wondered if Kitty had any additional insight. Not that it would matter much in the case against her father. She didn't know it yet, but the condemning evidence wasn't to be found here, but rather in Sam McGuire's financial records—or in this case, lack thereof. Luke wasn't convinced Sam was a murderer, either, but he'd been up to something illegal. He'd give Alec a call at the Bureau this afternoon and see how the financial trace was progressing. The sudden increase of funds into Sam's accounts over the last two years came from somewhere.

He rubbed his cheek where Kitty had kissed him yesterday. Eventually he needed to divulge information about her father that she was going to hate, but first he had to be sure she wasn't an unwitting pawn in SOLO's deadly games. He understood Kitty's loyalty to her father, but sometimes love caused one to be blind. He'd fallen into the same dark trap and almost lost everyone precious to him. With God's help, he'd never let down his guard again.

Sunlight danced across the ceiling. Kitty sighed, deliciously snug, wavering between sleep and wakefulness. She stretched her arms over her head, enjoying the cheerful chirping of birds wafting in with the fresh mountain air.

She rolled over and gasped at the sight of Luke slumped in a rocking chair outside her door. A Bible lay open on his lap, but his thick black lashes fanned tightly shut above his chiseled cheekbones. A gentle snore whistled through his open mouth. Kitty couldn't help smiling. He looked rather cute with his dark hair tousled and so much younger without the seriousness that lined his face during the day.

He moved, groaning softly. The chair had to be miserable to sleep in, and he'd stayed there all morning in an effort to . What? Protect her? No one had ever offered that before, not even her ex-fiancé. Obviously, she'd never actually needed protection and made it clear to people she could take of herself, but.… A strange sensation flowed through her like warm honey. Was this what it felt like to be cherished?

Disturbed by the vulnerability that question evoked, she shifted her gaze out the window. The Sierra's gray and white peaks soared sharply into the milky blue of the cloud-laced sky. She and Dad backpacked those mountains on one of the rare vacations he'd taken. Other shorter trips had been under-taken with Evan and other kids, supervised by the church's youth leaders. Even though she resisted being a regular member, she'd been invited along those first couple of years. It was the one good memory she had of the church.

When footsteps padded overhead, she realized Michael must be awake. He'd pulled a fast one last night by disengag-ing the intercom. Much as the prank annoyed her, she couldn't feel too self-righteous. She'd always been sneaking out and heading for big trouble until her father finally decided it was safer just to let her tag after him while he worked. Hanging out at the fire station had been surprisingly exhilarating, and she'd come to think of the guys as extended family. The expe-rience changed her life and influenced her choice of career. She still felt more at home at the fire station than anywhere else.

A robin landed on the deck railing and puffed out his red chest, proudly displaying a worm dangling from his beak. Time for her to get busy too. Kitty slid from the bed and spied her duffel bag lying by the door with Luke's bare foot propped on top. Her stomach dropped.

The note.

She'd left the note about weapons inside the bag. She glanced at the Bible on Luke's lap. He didn't strike her as a man who'd rifle through her things while she slept. But then, what did she know about him, really? The warmth she'd felt earlier seeped away, replaced by cold common sense. She had to remember Tanner wasn't her friend. He had a job to do, and so did she.

She inched close enough to catch his scent of soap and musk. There was no way to get the bag without moving his foot. She cleared her throat. When he didn't stir, she poked his shoulder.

"You're awake," Luke said, stretching, one hand grabbing his neck. "Ouch. What time is it?"

Kitty lifted her watch and noticed with dismay that soot blackened her wrist. She got a whiff of wood smoke. "It's about ten after eleven. I need a shower before I head to the ravine."

"Fine. I'll check to see if Michael's up." Luke unbent himself from the chair, and dragged it to a corner in the room.

"I heard him a minute ago." Kitty picked up her duffel bag, relieved to find the zipper still closed.

"How are you feeling?"

"Better. Thanks." At least her head had stopped throbbing. She didn't mention the band of tension in her chest that tightened with each passing minute.

She showered quickly and threw on khaki shorts and a white tank top embroidered with the emblem of her fire agency. As she picked up her discarded jeans to pack them away, something clunked on the floor. It was the pyrite rock she'd found in her father's desk. She'd meant to put it with her father's collection at the cabin yesterday. She held the glittering fool's gold up in the sunlight. The sparkling mineral felt good in her hand, a solid memory of the few times they'd spent together combing the mountains and riverbanks searching for it.

"I miss you, Dad," she whispered before shoving the rock into her back pocket. Determination filled her. So far, almost everything that had happened over the last twenty-four hours supported her conviction of her father's innocence. Only the note she'd found last night bothered her. What had her father meant by it? She needed to examine the note again and make a copy before she handed it over to Luke and the sheriff.

She dug through her clothes in the bag, but the paper wasn't where'd she left it.

Acid churned in her stomach. Where was it?

She locked the door and turned the bag over on her bed, dumping the contents. Her fingers shook as she methodically examined every item until she packed everything away again.

Light-headed, she perched on the bed. This couldn't be happening. Surely, she hadn't imagined finding the scrap of paper. She examined the sliding door to the deck, and the security bar was solidly set. That meant someone who had access to the house must've come into her room and pawed through her things.

Her heart raced. As mysteriously as it had arrived, the note had vanished.

Kitty stared out the Bronco window as Luke drove into town. They'd dropped off Michael at school. He'd actually been eager to go, probably to tell his classmates about his adventure the previous night.

A few people strolled along Main Street, stopping to chit-chat, window shop or gaze at the glittering lake. Next week when the autumn leaves hit their peak, more tourists would arrive in time for the Fall Festival. The three-day event provided a welcome income for the town before the lull of the winter months. High hopes for profitable winter trade had been burned, along with the ski resort. Tourists would continue to bypass their little town for the beckoning ski hills of Mammoth or June Lake.

They rolled past Liz's Arts and Crafts. On the other side of the sparkling window, Elizabeth Greene held a basket of dried flowers and chatted with a customer. Could she be the one who found the incriminating note? She carried a key and she'd been there early this morning fixing breakfast. Somehow, Kitty couldn't imagine Elizabeth sneaking into the bedroom and snooping through her duffel bag. What motive would she have? Surely she didn't see Kitty as a threat. Not when Elizabeth was so comfortably ensconced in the Tanner family.

Kitty suspected the thief sat next to her, his finger tapping the steering wheel as he waited for the car ahead of them to make a left. But why hadn't he said anything?

Luke drove past the sports store where Jeremy worked and zipped into a parking space in front of Sarah's Café.

"I thought we were heading for the ravine," Kitty said.

"We are. I called ahead to have Sarah pack us lunch. You can go pick it up while I hang the banner for the festival. It should only take about ten minutes."

"Inherited that job from my dad, huh?"

"Yep. That's what happens when you carry a ladder."

She jumped from the truck and trotted up the steps. The café door jangled, and a savory aroma greeted her as she entered the empty dining room. A cooler waited by the cash register.

"Sarah?" Kitty called.

Daniel Moore ambled out of the kitchen, wiping his hands with a large white towel. "She's not here. Will I do?"

"You bet." Kitty hugged her father's old friend and kissed his weathered cheek. "What smells so good?"

"Venison stew."

"You get the deer?"

"Nope, Sarah bagged this one and froze the meat last fall. I'm stew-watching while she's at the grocery, persuading Joe into ordering some kind of fancy herbs. She'll skin *my* hide if I let tonight's special burn."

Kitty chuckled with him but with less enthusiasm. Sarah's temper could be fierce. Her father used to purposely tease Sarah just to see her erupt, but Kitty chose to disappear when Sarah let her tongue fly.

"Want to sample a bowlful?" The gold in Daniel's lower front tooth flashed as he smiled.

"I'm sure the stew's wonderful, but no thanks." She'd never acquired a taste for venison. Maybe it was because she just couldn't get Bambi's image out of her mind. "Tanner ordered some sandwiches to pick up. He's in the street hanging the festival banner."

He gestured toward the cash register. "They're in the cooler. Sarah put in chips and her special German potato salad too. Where are you headed?"

"Wildcat Ravine."

Daniel's grin faded. "You sure you're up to it?"

"No," she answered truthfully, "but I need to go. I have so many questions no one can seem to answer. Like why did he go to the ravine in the first place? Was there smoke? Did he spot anyone suspicious? And why didn't he call it in?"

"If I knew, I'd tell you, honey." He grabbed a pitcher marked Iced Tea and poured the tea into chilled glasses. "Come, let's sit by the window."

Kitty tasted the tea, dumped in sugar and stirred it vigorously. He waited until she took another sip and asked, "How's your grandmother? We sure miss her visits."

"Doing okay, considering she's wheelchair bound. I talked to her this morning. She sends her regards."

"How'd she take the news?"

"I didn't tell her about the cabin," Kitty said, fighting a sense of guilt. It would be such a relief to share this burden with someone, but the fragile woman didn't need anything else to fret over. "Losing Dad was hard on her."

"Wish I could've been there last night. I had an emergency plumbing job on one of those fancy houses on the ridge. Cracked pipe. Owners haven't been up for a year. Must not have drained them, and they froze. All it took was a surge in pressure, and kaboom. Flooded the first floor." His liver-spotted hand patted hers. "If you need a place to stay, child, you're welcome at our house."

She gazed out the window. Luke stood on a ladder tying up the rope stringing the banner across Main Street. Most likely, she'd worn out her welcome at the Tanner house, but if she stayed with the Greenes, Sarah would grill her on every detail…and watch her every move. "Thank you—I appreciate the offer. I'll let you know. Right now, I'm just living moment to moment."

Daniel nodded as if he understood her reluctance. She'd always found it hard to believe this laid-back mountain man and the feisty, impeccable Sarah were married. Daniel dressed in faded overalls and a red-and-black flannel shirt with the sleeves rolled up. A battered pipe poked out of his bib pocket, but he rarely lit it, in compliance with Sarah's smoking ban. Both he and Sam with his cigars made several attempts over the years to quit. Daniel still hung on to his one bad vice, as he called it. So had her father, apparently, if one gave any credence to the rumor of his cigar starting the Wildcat fire.

Daniel lifted his coffee and took a noisy sip. He was a man of few words when Sarah was around. He said she did enough talking for the both of them. However, Daniel could be a virtual fountain of information if someone got him alone. Today, he seemed positively chatty.

"Rumor has it you're working for Tanner."

"That's right."

"Hmm." He stroked the gray whiskers on his chin. "Sad he and his son are all alone in the world. A grandfather's no substitute for a wife and mother."

Kitty sputtered into her iced tea. "Daniel, you're not trying to play matchmaker, are you?"

"Me?" Daniel went wide-eyed with mock innocence. "No, I leave that stuff to Sarah."

"Well, I wouldn't be surprised if she put you up to it."

"She worries about you." He sighed. "She worries about everything these days."

"Well, she doesn't have to worry about me."

"Heard about your possible promotion to arson investigation. Your dad would've been proud."

"Maybe." Probably not, though. Not once had her father ever uttered those words to her. "Daniel, I need to know something. Was Dad acting strangely before the fire?"

He set down his empty glass. His finger traced his pipe stem as if he longed to light it. "Sam stuck his nose into a lot of things going on in this town, and it isn't my place to judge him or his politics."

"Politics? What do you mean?"

A pot clanged in the kitchen and Daniel jumped. "Sounds like Clarence's here. Guess I can get back to the hardware store. But Kitty—" he leaned forward, lowering his voice "—I may not have agreed with your father at times, but I respected him. I know you two butted heads those last few years, but that isn't an excuse. Sheer stubbornness from both of you kept you apart. He sure missed you."

"How was I supposed to know?" A knot tightened in her throat. "He could've called and told me."

"Something wrong with *your* fingers, girl?"

Kitty winced at the truth in his words. "You're right, but I can't change the past. I can only focus on proving Dad's innocence and protecting Nana from vicious rumors." She took a deep breath, steeling herself for what his answer might be. "Those politics Dad was involved in…was it with a group called SOLO?"

Daniel's jaw clenched. "Guess it's no secret now. Yes, he belonged and so did I."

EIGHT

"They found the Bronco here," Luke said, killing the engine. Kitty gazed around the graveled clearing, empty except for a lone, dusty car near the National Forest sign informing hikers the trail to Wildcat Falls was a mile.

Kitty hopped out of the truck, gravel crunching under her hiking boots. She'd spent the time on the drive over the winding dirt road trying not to hyperventilate. Until now, she'd chosen to believe her father hadn't been actively involved in an organization some people referred to as eco-terrorists. SOLO did stand for national conservation, and it was unfortunate a subgroup within the membership brought down the organization. Those who remained connected to SOLO were deemed a radical fringe.

Daniel told her he had accompanied Sam to the quarterly meetings in Sacramento but assured her that after the arson in Colorado, he'd severed ties. If Sam remained involved, Daniel didn't reveal any reasons. He just assured her Sam would've never done anything crazy. SOLO kept current membership confidential, so how the sheriff and Chief Tanner discovered the connection remained a mystery. Daniel surmised they had high connections somewhere.

She'd been so shocked to learn about SOLO, she'd forgotten to ask Daniel about her father's sudden interest in the church. Were the events related? Was her father seeking atonement for a huge sin?

She shuddered. No. Despite the secrets her father seemed to have, she didn't believe he was capable of arson. His honor and love for the land wouldn't let him do such a heinous thing. Something else was going on and she would get to the bottom of it. Maybe Wildcat Ravine held the answers.

Kitty cut a sideways look at Luke, who leaned on the back bumper, changing his boots for hiking shoes. What were *his* secrets?

He was probably the one who'd rummaged through her things and taken the note. But if he hadn't, she didn't want to alert him to the fact of its existence yet. Not until she knew who could be trusted.

She glanced around the parking lot again. Time to get to work. "Which way was the truck facing? In or out?"

"In. Like we are now."

A wave of disappointment hit her. Her dad would've turned the Bronco out toward the road if he'd seen smoke or thought he'd need a quick getaway. Either he'd been here for pleasure, or he'd been too distracted to follow safe protocol.

"Were the doors locked?" she asked.

He nodded and lifted two green day packs out of the cargo area and handed one to Kitty. "Ready?"

No, but she nodded anyway. He set a brisk pace on the gated service road. The tire-wide ruts narrowed to a steep footpath as they climbed over a rocky rise and traversed across the mountain face. Although the breeze blew cool, the sun seared the top her forehead. When they stopped at the halfway point, she yanked her ponytail higher off her damp neck and took a long swig of bottled water.

Luke waited patiently a few feet away, gazing out across the valley toward Pine Lake. The wind ruffled his dark hair, sunlight turning it to ebony. His stance radiated confidence, a man secure in his surroundings. For someone who'd lived here less than a year, he seemed to have more of a bond to this place than she'd ever felt growing up here. And now the one place she could've called home lay in ashes.

It shouldn't matter so much. Moving to L.A. to be nearer to Nana and the last location she lived with her mother, had been a good decision, but did she really feel a connection there? Her apartment was just a place to sleep. She spent most of her time taking classes or working, always in constant change. Even her engagement to Jordan lacked a feeling of solidity. Maybe that's why she hadn't been totally surprised when things had turned sour.

"We better get a move on." Luke's deep voice broke into her thoughts. He'd caught her staring at him again, but she was too depressed to care. She turned abruptly and took the lead over the next rise. Blackened trees, bent and twisted, stood as a testimony to the inferno that'd swept the mountainside. The lingering scent of charred wood tickled her nose.

Luke pointed to one side of Wildcat Ravine where the fire had ignited and raced east across the mountain, consuming the new buildings at the ski resort before hungrily devouring the thick forest behind the town. Only a sudden wind shift had saved the downtown stores and homes.

Kitty stepped over a charred log. Eventually, time would hide the injury caused to the forest. Even now, small splashes of green, new life sprung forth to cover the dead remains. Nature's way. If only it were as simple to ease heartache.

Ahead, water bubbled and swirled over the rocks with a gleeful sound before plunging over the edge of Wildcat Falls. Kitty eased down between the boulders to the stream, welcoming a rush of damp, cool air.

Pyrite bits sparkled gold along the bank and under the water. She and Evan used to pretend they'd discovered a pirate's treasure trove. Larger mineral chunks lay farther up the mountain near the abandoned mines where her father probably collected the rock she still carried in her pocket.

"They found the kerosene canister about twenty feet up the stream." Luke's voice brought reality crashing back. "The same kind they found near your cabin."

"And the cigar butt?"

"Found a couple feet back from where you're standing. Cigarette butts too. Among those rocks." He pointed to an outcropping hanging over the waterfall.

"Then it wasn't what started the fire."

"Never said it did. The report revealed the cigar was fairly fresh and intact." Luke set his day pack down and squatted near the stream's edge, his gaze on the rippling water. "I'm sorry. I realize this must be hard for you."

Kitty clenched her teeth until her jaw ached as she inched past the Danger sign to the cliff's edge. The ravine spread out below, a jagged wound cut in the earth. Beautiful, but treacherous. The water barely covered her boot sole as she stepped near the drop-off. Grasping a nearby tree root, she leaned over the edge to see below. According to the report, they'd found Sam's battered body at the falls' base, an image that haunted her dreams.

She stared at the moss-covered rocks fifty feet beneath her boots. Nothing had changed. The small circle of clear glacier water beckoned invitingly. The trickle of water sounded soothing and peaceful in the fall. Birds twittered and darted through the canyon. A dank earthly odor rose from the pit, once enjoyable, but now the smell only reminded her of the graveyard where'd they'd lowered Sam's coffin into the ground.

Luke grabbed her arm and yanked her backward. "What are you doing?"

"Don't ever sneak up on someone like that! I could've fallen," Kitty said, shaking off his grip.

"You were swaying."

"So? My feet were securely on the ground. I'm not suicidal—I'm too angry. Besides, look at this. See all the roots and handholds? I could climb down the face fairly easy, and I don't even rock climb as a hobby." She glared at him. "Do you know there've only been a couple other accidents up here in the last fifteen years? And those were people who'd fallen in high water. The only other way straight down is if you wanted to jump."

Something flickered in Luke's eyes.

Indignation swelled, nearly choking her. "Oh, come on, Tanner, my father wouldn't have jumped."

"People do extraordinary things when feeling trapped."

She spread her arms wide. "The fire didn't even get close to here. He was a firefighter. He wouldn't have been afraid."

"I wasn't talking about that kind of trapped."

Kitty's mind refused to process the implication. "Not possible. Elizabeth saw my father at prayer meeting the night before and he seemed normal. If he were under that kind of stress, she would've noticed." She spun away. "I'm going to climb down to the bottom."

"Wait." He retrieved his pack and squeezed behind her through a narrow opening between two wet boulders.

He snagged her wrist as she stepped over rocks along a narrow path that snaked down along the cliff. She halted. "I don't need your help."

"Well, maybe I need yours," he said, squeezing her hand and sending tingles up her arm. "I'm a city boy."

She rolled her eyes. An unlikely excuse, but actually his strong grip felt good, reassuring, an anchor in the swirling sea of her emotions. He held on tightly until they'd sidled down the trail and reached the pool.

She cupped the water, splashing the dust off her face and neck, before gazing at the outcropping she'd stood on moments before. A chill shook her. "He could've been pushed."

Luke pressed his lips together and waited a beat. "We considered it, but there's no evidence of anyone else being up here. Photos taken from the fire tower only show the Bronco in the parking lot."

"They could've hiked in from another direction. Hid their car in the forest."

"The only way out would've been directly in the fire's path."

"There's one other way—through the ravine. I've gone out that way before. It's slow-going and dangerous with lots of crevices and loose earth but doable."

"If someone had gone out the ravine, then fire personnel would've already been stationed at the bottom and blocked the road. They would've seen anyone suspicious leaving the area."

"Not if he blended in," Kitty said, the implication hitting her as she came to the same conclusion she read in his eyes. If the arsonist was a firefighter, he could've slipped right into place. In the chaos of arriving personnel, no one would've noticed. "You already thought of the possibility, haven't you?"

Luke rubbed the back of his neck. "Stan checked it out. Everyone was accounted for…except your father."

Her gaze swept the rocky abyss to the startling azure sky, unable to find her voice. She rejected the idea that any of the honorable firemen she'd grown up with would harm her father. If not them, then who?

She sank down on a log, trying to get a grip on the emotions that rocked her. She'd expected something else. Maybe sorrow, maybe tears, not the helpless fury pulsing through her, shaking her to the core. No place so beautiful should be the scene of someone's death.

An eagle's cry floated from the clouds and then the sharp gun report echoed. A ping sounded over her head and tiny rocks trickled down the bank.

"Hey! Knock it off! There're people up here," she shouted, her voice bouncing on the sheer walls. She stood, scanning the top of the ravine.

Another bullet zinged by, closer this time. "Take cover!" Luke shouted.

She lunged across the stream with Luke and dove under a large, overhanging rock.

"Either they're really stupid or nearsighted or they're deliberately shooting at us." He yanked out his radio. "No signal. Why is it whenever I'm in a crisis with you, we're in a hole?"

"Lucky, I guess." Kitty's hand trembled as she checked her cell phone. No bars. Another gunshot boomed through the canyon. Luke peered around the boulder. "If we take the main trail, we'll be open targets."

"Targets?" Kitty's voice squeaked.

"You said you knew the way down the ravine."

"Yeah, b-but it's been years."

"What happened to all that confidence you had a few minutes ago?"

"I didn't expect to get shot at."

He pushed her forward. "Stay low. Go." They scrambled out from behind the rock, splashed through the stream and slid over a long rock into the crack of the lower ravine.

Boulders left from an ancient glacier towered over them and beneath their feet. The walls melded together in places and closed out the sky and any stray bullets. Now that they were safe from overzealous hunters, Kitty concentrated on finding safe footing in the shadows. One slip could send them sprawling into a black hole, breaking bones. Last time she'd traversed the ravine, Evan led the way. Although she hadn't believed him when he'd whispered the crevices were bottomless pits, she didn't want to find out how deep they really were.

The ravine snaked and split into deceptive fractures, leading to dead ends. The trick to success was to follow the main flow of the stream, even though it meant climbing down two smaller waterfalls and squeezing between rock walls. By the time they emerged into the woods by the lake, they were muddy, scratched and bruised but relatively unharmed.

"Nice job, McGuire," Luke said, his grin vivid on a dust-coated face. "A couple times there, I'd thought we'd have to backtrack."

So had she. "Thanks for your faith in me. I know it must've been hard."

He chuckled, and then his attention focused on her head. His eyes widened and he reached out, batting at her hair.

"What?" She shrieked.

"You don't want to know."

She shuddered and checked her clothes for any eight-legged hitchhikers as Luke radioed the shooting report to the dispatcher at the Communication Center. Skirting the lake's rocky edge, they circled back to Luke's truck to discover two neat bullet holes in the windshield. Kitty put her finger in one. "A warning?" she tried to ask lightly, but the words stuck to the roof of her dry mouth.

"Get in," Luke said, jumping into the driver's seat. He roared across the now-empty lot and down the road for about a mile before sliding to a halt by the lake. The squawking radio indicated he'd finally been patched through to the sheriff. He quickly recounted the events of the last two hours as he used a pocket knife to extract a bullet from the vinyl seat.

"No, Stan, I didn't think it was a good idea to wait there." He glanced at Kitty and grimaced. "Right. We're heading to Tower 122, and I'll meet you at the church tonight."

Kitty leaned forward, her arms wrapped around her. The bullets had blasted holes into the vinyl where their heads would've been.

They'd parked below the ravine, the tiny waterfall far above them. She scanned the mountainside, blackened and bare, devoid of movement. Luke reached under the seat and pulled out binoculars. She rolled her window down and listened, almost breathless, but the only sounds were the wind in the trees and the distant lapping of the lake.

"If they had any sense, they're long gone," Kitty said.

Luke lowered the binoculars, his expression grim. "Who says they have sense?"

Luke's fingers strangled the steering wheel, his foot heavy on the gas as he concentrated on maintaining maximum speed without sliding on the hairpin curves. Kitty gripped the overhand support, her alert gaze trained on the passing scenery. Tension vibrated between them.

At last they reached the peak and parked below the metal forest service tower. Luke shoved his door open. "Ron's on duty today, and he was up here the day your father died. He called in the fire."

"I know...I spoke with him at the funeral," Kitty replied, leading the way to the base of the ladder.

Filth covered her jeans and shirt, mud caked her hiking boots and scratches streaked her arms from climbing over the boulders but not once had she complained as she led them to safety. And despite what must be a very emotional ordeal, she'd taken in the details of her father's demise with professionalism. His admiration for her grew.

Luke suspected Sam might not have been alone on the cliff, but with no proof, he couldn't jump to conclusions. He was certain of one thing, though. Sam McGuire had dragged his daughter into danger. The bullets Luke dug out of his car weren't ordinarily used for hunting, at least not for animals. They'd come from a high-powered rifle. The type snipers used. Who in Pine Lake had access to such a powerful weapon, and why were they shooting at them?

Dear God, I need help with this one. What is going on?

"Hi, folks, come on up." Ranger Ronald Wilson leaned over the railing high above their heads. "Sheriff radioed you were on your way."

"Ladies first." Luke gestured to a long metal ladder. Kitty swung onto the rungs and scurried up. He followed closely, and she almost trod on his head a few times.

"The climb seems to get longer every year. Keeps these middle-aged legs of mine in shape." Ron guffawed and gave Kitty a hug. "Great to see you, Miss Kitty. I've missed you. Are you here to stay for a bit?"

"Only for a short time. I need to get back to L.A. after I wrap some things up here." She glanced at Luke. His breath caught. Was there a tinge of regret in her blue eyes? And why did he suddenly feel sorry at the thought of her leaving? Life would be peaceful again. Just what he wanted. Only now... peaceful sounded boring.

"Sheriff filled me in on why you're here," Ron said. "Sorry I didn't hear the rifle shots. Wind's blowing the wrong way, or I might have been inside." He lifted a high-powered scope hanging from a hook on the wall and handed it over. Luke zoomed in on the dark ribbon of Wildcat Ravine that sliced the mountain base, but nothing moved on the trails. The falls' parking lot remained empty.

He passed the scope to the Kitty. "I don't think we're dealing with an ordinary poacher. He blew holes in my windshield with a rifle, and from the sound of the shots, they came from quite a distance."

Ron let loose a low whistle. "Forestry will cooperate any way we can."

"There's something else." Luke glanced at Kitty. The dry wind whipped around her, painting rosy color onto her cheeks. Her unusual passivity worried him. What was she plotting now? "I know you've been over this at least a dozen times, but Kitty would like to hear your impressions of what you saw around the time of the Wildcat fire."

"I figured as much. Heard about all the goings-on in town." Ron ambled over to Kitty and leaned on the railing beside her. "Your dad stopped by the day before the fire and sat out here with me for a while. Told me you were taking classes in arson investigation. Seemed right proud."

Kitty lowered the scope. "He did?"

"Oh, yeah. In fact, he shared quite a few memories with me. Talked about how you used to tag after him all those years and how much he missed those days. He wished things could've been different so he wouldn't have regrets."

She swallowed. "Regrets about what?"

"I don't know. Guys don't get into deep discussions about feelings. I assume he referred to the things all parents worry about. Did they do a good enough job? Will their kids be safe and happy?" He shrugged. "Mine have all gotten married and have lives of their own, but I still worry. It never stops."

"That's for sure," Luke murmured, checking his watch. School had dismissed and Michael should be at the church with his granddad, assuming he hadn't landed in detention again.

"I never saw Sam again." Ron continued. "The next afternoon, I spotted smoke above the falls. The wind blew something fierce. Next thing we knew, we were dealing with a firestorm. Headed straight for the construction site at the resort. We sent out a warning, but two hotel workers got caught in a flash-fire and didn't make it out."

"You spotted the initial smoke at 1530 hours?" Luke asked.

"Let me check." He went inside and returned with a log-book. "Yep, 1531 is when I logged the first sighting. Took photographs and turned the video camera on. From the photos, you could make out Sam's truck in the parking lot. 'Course, at the time, I thought he'd responded to the call. I didn't know he'd been up at the falls. I'm sorry, Kitty."

"You have no reason to be sorry. How could you have known?" she said in strangled voice. "Apparently, nobody did."

"Could we see the video, Ron?" Luke asked. "We're retracing Sam's steps those last two days. We thought she might have a difference perspective than the investigators."

"Wish I could. Don't have a copy up here. Lightning hit the computer line about a month back. Some idiot bypassed the surge protector. The sheriff asked me for another copy last week, but the hard drive fried."

Interesting. What was Johnson onto now? "Another copy? Did he say why?"

"Nope. I told him to check with the county office or D.A. Sorry," Ron said.

"That's okay, I'll—"

"But you always keep a copy of your own at home, don't you, Ron?" Kitty interrupted, placing her hand on his arm.

His face creased into a sheepish smile. "You remembered? Just goes to show little pitchers have big ears."

"Luke won't get you into trouble. He can keep secrets." She leveled her blue eyes at him.

He raised an eyebrow. Which secret was she referring to?

"Not that there's any reason someone should care if you keep souvenirs," she continued, her attention back on Ron. "You should see Dad's scrapbooks."

Ron shifted uneasily. "I wouldn't call this a souvenir, but I do like to keep my own private records, just in case anyone ever questions my conduct. I got accused a long time ago of not doing my job properly. Similar situation—people died. The only visual record disappeared. Now I use my own camera too. It's not like I stole anything."

"I understand. Don't worry about it," Luke said. He'd already investigated Ron and knew about the dismissed negligence charges. People were always trying to pin the blame on someone. The fact the man kept copies of everything might come in handy someday.

"Tell you what," Ron said, "I'll run down to the house and burn you a DVD, if you don't mind standing watch for twenty minutes or so."

"You're my hero, Ron." Kitty kissed him on the cheek.

The older man blushed. "Tell my missus next time you see her, okay?" He shot down the ladder and jumped in his Jeep.

Luke turned to Kitty. "Hero?"

She lifted one shoulder. "Anyone who tries to help my father is a hero in my book.

"What about me? I'm here, aren't I? Am I a hero?" He'd meant it in jest, but suddenly her answer mattered to him.

"That remains to be seen." The wind tugged wisps of hair out of her ponytail as she turned her gaze to the mountain again.

"Okay, what's bugging you? Other than—"

She spun to face him, hands on hips. "Other than what? What could be bugging me? Let me see. What should I wish for? That my father clumsily fell off a cliff on a trail he'd been on a thousand times? Or maybe someone he trusted pushed him? Or worse yet, he became so distraught over his life, he committed suicide?"

"You don't have to be sarcastic," Luke said. "I know you're frustrated."

"We are no further along than the day I got here." Her face

flamed. "I want answers! What are you hiding from me? I can't trust anyone, not even you."

"Trust has to go both ways. I've been as honest with you as I can be under the circumstances."

"What's that's supposed to mean?" Her chest heaved, her breath coming in gasps.

"Calm down. You're going to hyperventilate." He stepped closer. They'd taught him how to take down criminals at the FBI academy, but he was pretty sure they hadn't taught a class on how to handle beautiful, hysterical firefighters.

He took her hand with the pretense of checking her pulse, the beat rapid beneath hot skin. "I want answers too."

She looked up at him, her eyes bright, almost feverish. "Yeah, so you can close the case. You don't care about my father or me."

Luke went still as the realization slammed into him. He did care. He cared too much. This was bad. Very bad. He placed a hand on her shoulder.

"Just leave me alone!" She jerked away from him and burst into tears.

Kitty covered her face with her hands, mortified as the sobs hiccupped out of her. Luke patted her awkwardly, which only made her cry harder as the dam of pent-up frustration and sorrow finally burst.

Luke muttered something incomprehensible and pulled her into his strong, capable arms, smoothing her hair with his hand. She stiffened and then relaxed in his embrace, her ear on his chest. His heart beat strong and steady, slowly calming her. The sobs subsided to weeping, then sniffles. She scrubbed her face with her hand.

"I'm sorry." She stepped away, and cool air rushed between them.

He shrugged. "Nothing wrong with shedding a few tears."

A few tears? Kitty studied the large wet spot on his shirt and smiled with trembling lips. "I don't cry very often, especially not in public. My father despised tears. Thought it showed weakness."

"That's a matter of opinion."

"Really?" Kitty asked in a skeptical tone. "I bet you don't cry in public."

He didn't answer for several seconds, his hands clamped tightly on the railing. "Maybe not on the outside, but I'm familiar with heartache."

His bleak expression tugged at her soul. "I'm sorry. I don't know what you've been through and have no right to judge." She touched his shoulder. "Someone told me you're a widower. I can't imagine how hard it would be. You know, if you ever want to talk about it, I'm... Well, I figure after sobbing all over your shirt, the least I can do is to shut up and listen for a change."

When he didn't answer, her fingers squeezed his biceps. "Seriously, I promise I won't tell anyone if you want to cry out loud."

A smile tugged at his lips and laughter spilled out. He turned toward her, shaking his head. "You know, out of all the offers of a sympathetic ear from women in Pine Lake, yours is the most unique."

"Sorry, couldn't help it." She grinned. "I've never been able to stay sentimental for long. I guess that makes me immature."

"Well, don't lose whatever it is that makes you smile like that." He gently cupped her face, and his thumb brushed her damp cheek. "I barely know you, and the time we've spent together has been rather disastrous, but you're starting to grow on me."

"Is this a good thing?"

"The jury is still out." He leaned closer and gazed into her eyes.

The whole forest could be burning down behind him, and she wouldn't be able to move. Was this a test? Did he want to kiss her? Should she let him?

Her mind whirled at the implications, and then out of nowhere, a loud hiccup erupted. Her fingers fluttered to her mouth. "Oops."

Luke leaned away, his eyes twinkling. "You never fail to entertain."

Her face heated. Why was this man destined to see her at her worst? She shouldn't care, but she did. Luke had been courageous, saving Max and trying to protect her. Could he be different from Jordan? Could she actually trust him?

She took a deep breath. "You said trust has to go both ways."

"Yeah." Luke answered, his gaze trained on the forest below.

"Can I trust you?" she asked.

"Sure."

Kitty rolled her eyes skyward at his flip tone. "No, I mean, really trust that if I tell you something that might be considered incriminating to my father, you'll keep an open mind."

"What is it?" he said, now watching her like a mountain lion stalking prey.

She sighed with resignation. "I found a note in my duffel bag last night. You must have scooped it up in my clothes at the cabin."

Luke reached into his back pocket and extracted a plastic bag containing a torn piece of paper. "Like this?"

She stared at the familiar handwriting with outrage. "I

knew it! You went through my bag while I was sleeping? You stole it from me. And you just said I could trust you!"

"Hey I—"

A car honked below them. Kitty gritted her teeth as Ron climbed the ladder. She'd been right. Luke had violated her privacy. Betrayal rolled over her. And to think, minutes ago she'd almost kissed him!

"Sorry I took so long," Ron said, carrying a manila envelope in his hand. "Here are my notes on the fire and the digital recording." He paused, his gaze shifting between them. "Everything all right?"

"Just fine," Luke said. "Would you mind if I hang on to these for a little while?"

"Keep 'em. Those are copies."

Luke glanced at his watch. "We better go. How about a chess game next week if things calm down?"

Ron's face crinkled into a smile. "Sounds good. Will you be around for the festival, Kitty?"

"Not if she can help it," Luke said as he stepped onto the ladder.

Shooting a glare at Luke, she gave Ron a hug. "I hope I see you again before I go."

"I'm off next weekend, so maybe at church?"

"Maybe," she said, although she fervently hoped she was back home by then. The only reason she'd set foot in that church again would be for the investigation.

"Thanks for everything." She waved to Ron and scurried down the ladder, diving into the truck as Luke revved the engine. They tore down the dirt road until he brought the pickup to an abrupt stop under a grove of skinny pine trees.

He turned toward her. "For your information, I found this note in your dad's cabin. I didn't go through your bag, although I'm thinking now that might not be a bad idea. I assume you have the other half? You want to tell me why you withheld possible evidence?"

Kitty's face burned. "Hey, you withheld information from me too."

"As I said, trust has to go both ways." He dangled the plastic bag in front of her.

Kitty's shoulders drooped. "Okay, you have a point. I just wanted to make a copy of the note before I turned it over. I figured I might never see it again."

"Plausible answer. Here—just don't get your fingerprints on it." He handed her the bag.

"This does look like the other half of the one I found in my duffel bag last night."

"Which, I assume from what you said, is missing?"

"You don't have to sound so cynical." She held the note higher to catch the sunlight before it disappeared behind the Four Sisters.

out of the field neither cut down
for
with fire and they shall spoil them that spoiled them
aith the Lord God
39:10

"Turn it over," Luke said.

Kitty flipped the paper, revealing her father's handwriting again.

I have fulfilled my side of the bargain. It is time—

"What did your piece say?" he asked, his gaze intent.

She hesitated. "Something about burning weapons." She handed the note back. "I know the wording sounds bad under the circumstances, but remember, jotting down Bible texts isn't against the law. There's probably a perfectly good explanation."

"Was your father in the habit of typing out Biblical texts?"

Kitty bit her lower lip. "I didn't think Dad even owned a Bible. When I lived here, he went to church when it suited him, which was maybe once or twice a year on the holidays. But according to your father and Elizabeth, that all changed." She shifted in her seat, unable to get comfortable. "The reference started with E. Maybe the text was part of a Bible study."

Luke released the brake and they rolled forward. "Maybe, but I want the other half of the note. It has to be in the house somewhere."

"Right," Kitty said, although she wouldn't count on it. Her life had taken on a surreal quality, and logic didn't apply. Unseen assailants, vanishing pinecones, snipers…what next?

"We'll go by the house on the way."

She rubbed the back of her aching neck and picked off a piece of gravel.

"On the way to where?"

"Prayer meeting."

NINE

"Kitty, I'm glad you came tonight. You father would've been pleased," Pastor James said, balancing a small plate of lemon cake on his coffee mug. Behind him, a cheerful murmur of voices filled the fellowship hall as members partook of the local sweet bounty. Kitty set her fork down and contemplated a second helping of apple pie.

"I enjoyed the discussion on faith in the face of adversity," she said, ignoring the reference to her father. She still hadn't reconciled this unknown aspect of his life. "If I didn't know better, I'd think the topic was chosen specifically for me."

"Nice coincidence. I strive to present topics pertinent to the times."

Kitty snorted. "Elizabeth said you were supposed to be discussing spiritual gifts tonight."

He smiled good-naturedly. "She likes to keep me humble. I planned on covering enduring faith in a few weeks, but at the last moment, I felt inspired to bring it up tonight. I hope I didn't make you uncomfortable."

"Not really," she answered as a matronly looking woman tapped the reverend on the shoulder, drawing his attention away.

Kitty nibbled on a brownie. Considering she'd allegedly been shot at this afternoon and still reeled from the loss of her dad's cabin, the faith testimony of some members provided comfort. She shared a common bond with many who were also in pain, and she just wished she could reach the level of peace they had.

Sure, she believed in God, although she didn't involve Him in her everyday life. Needing a church used to seem like an unnecessary, weak indulgence, but now...something had changed with her father's death. Something seemed lacking in her life. She yearned for more. Had her father gone seeking more, too?

As a child she'd longed for that connection while at the same time she pushed away those that came too close. Rejection hurt too much, so why risk it? Even now, though she shared a camaraderie with the firefighters at work, she preferred to remain detached. Jordan had managed to batter down the wall she'd erected and then tried to change her into his perfect vision of a wife and mother. The same kind Luke and Michael needed.

She sighed, and her belt dug into her waist. She'd forego another piece of pie. She looked around with interest. The last time she'd been here, she still wore braces. The room grew more congested by the minute, as the several Bible classes held throughout the building dismissed and people congregated.

She scanned the milling crowd for Luke. After they'd unsuccessfully searched the guest bedroom and the house for the other half of the note, he met the sheriff in the church parking lot. Over an hour had passed since she'd snuck into the back of the fellowship hall for the class Luke said her father attended. She hadn't seen Luke or the sheriff since.

A girlish squeal sounded behind her. "Kitty McGuire? Is it really you?"

Kitty cringed and turned to find a vaguely familiar, stout, redhead with freckles. "Emma?"

"Oh, you remembered my name! How cool. And here's Charlotte and Lynn." More squeals. Kitty didn't recognize the other two women, but their voices nudged a vague recollection. Emma had been several years behind Kitty in school.

"Do you remember how much fun we had camping with the youth group?" Emma asked, plopping on the bench next to Kitty and linking arms. She didn't get a chance to answer as the three ladies chatted up a storm. Their warmth and energy soon coaxed Kitty into laughing.

"I hope you're going to be around for a while." Charlotte patted her round stomach beneath a floral blouse. "I'm due next month. This is my third."

"Are you going to be here for the Fall Festival?" Lynn stretched her lean, jean-clad legs over the adjoining bench.

"Maybe. I'm not sure how long I'll be here."

Emma leaned over and nudged Kitty's shoulder. "Did anyone tell you what a hoot your father was at prayer meeting? He told the best jokes, and he always asked the most interesting questions. He kept people squirming, but in a good way."

"I'm afraid I didn't even know he attended. Were you here at the meeting before the Wildcat fire?"

Emma refilled Kitty's coffee mug and shook her head. "I went to Butler to shop and got stuck in traffic coming home."

"We were here." Charlotte glanced at Lynn, and she nodded.

"I know this may be a strange question, but was my father acting unusual?"

Charlotte shrugged and then had to tug her top down over her baby bump. "Not that I noticed, other than I don't think he stayed for the whole thing. Wish I could remember more."

"I think he got a call," Lynn added, her forehead wrinkled with concentration. "I came down here to start the coffee and saw him out there in the parking lot. Then a car pulled up. Looked like the sheriff, but I didn't really pay attention. And I didn't see Sam the rest of the evening. In fact, that was the last time I ever saw him." Her brown eyes glistened, and she dug a tissue out of her bag. The other two ladies reached for tissues too.

"We miss him," Emma said with a sniff. She slung her arm over Kitty's shoulder.

Still raw from this afternoon, Kitty's emotions heaved. Soon, they'd have her crying again and this time in public. Luke waved from the doorway. "I have to go. Thanks for the talk," she said with relief.

Emma rose with her and gave her a hug. "If you're still here, come for church and sit with us. I'm so glad we can be friends again."

"Thank you." Kitty succumbed to warm hugs from the other ladies, and when she crossed the room to Luke, her eyes watered. He raised his eyebrows.

"I'm not crying."

He smiled. "Good. This is a clean shirt."

She followed him up the stairs to the quiet sanctuary and down the aisle to the front. On the left side of the platform, a door led to the pastor's study. Michael lay on his back on the rug balancing a tennis ball on his upturned feet. Jack sat beside him, ears cocked, watching the ball with interest. His yellow eyes glanced at Kitty as she entered the room.

James came around the desk, a Bible open in his hands. "I found the text you were searching for. It wasn't in Ecclesiastes like you thought, but in Ezekiel. He read, *"So they shall take no wood out of the field, neither cut down any out of the forests; for they shall burn the weapons with fire: and they shall spoil those that spoiled them, and rob those that robbed them, saith the Lord God."*

Luke glanced at Kitty. "Sounds like something a group like SOLO might embrace."

Kitty's chest constricted. That had been her fear.

James lowered the Bible. "You mean the nutty group who tie themselves to trees and lie in front of bulldozers?"

"Among other things," Luke said dryly. "I'd like a copy of the verse."

"I can print the chapter off the computer." James stepped around Michael to a desktop PC and clicked on the keyboard. "Just got the new laser printer set up yesterday."

The printer hummed and shot out a page. Kitty stared at it, a hunch forming in her mind. "Did you give that note to the sheriff yet?" she asked Luke.

"Nope. Johnson had to attend to a problem and wanted me to drop the bullets and note at the lab." Luke withdrew the plastic bag from his shirt pocket and handed it to her. "What do you want it for?"

"You'll see." She gingerly pulled a corner of the wrinkled paper out of the plastic bag, licked her fingertip and rubbed the type.

"Hey, stop that, you're tampering with evidence."

"Like people tromping all over it at the cabin didn't?" Kitty said, holding up the note. "Look, the ink smeared."

James peered over his spectacles. "So it did."

Luke scowled. "It smeared because you spit on it."

"Cool. Can I spit on it too?" Michael asked.

"No," Luke said. "No more spitting. What's your point, Kitty?"

"The newer inks don't smear this easily." Kitty grinned and relinquished the note to Luke. "I should know—I struggled all the way through school with a printer so ancient it should've been in the Smithsonian. The ink smeared if you even breathed on the page too heavily, and if you sneezed, your assignment was history. The printer finally died my junior year."

"But the printer in the station is a laser like this one," Luke pointed out.

"Exactly, and my dad didn't have a printer in the cabin. So most likely, he didn't print this note. All we have to do is match up the ink."

"I think you may be on to something there." Luke smiled at her with warm approval that made Kitty want to dance around the room.

"But—" his smile faded "—do you realize how many printers are in this town? Not to mention someone could've mailed the note to him from anywhere in the world."

"My son the pessimist," James said.

Kitty's shoulders slumped. "He's right—it'd take a miracle to find the right printer."

James grinned. "Well, you're in luck, my dear ones. I know Someone who specializes in miracles. Shall we pray?"

Kitty blew dust off the yellowed newspaper copy and watched Evan from her cross-legged position on the wooden floor of the *Tribune*'s storage room. He hefted a box filled with faded newsprint to the top of a stack of brown file boxes lining the wall. "Didn't Mr. Jenkins ever consider using microfilm or a computer? I'm surprised Dad didn't cite this closet as a fire hazard."

Evan snorted as he grabbed another box. "Jenkins's computer was so ancient, it still used five-inch floppies. One of these days I want to transfer the files on it, assuming I can get it to boot up again. Fortunately, Jenkins ran the paper as a monthly publication. So there's not as much to store. You're looking at thirty years in this tiny room."

"I wish I could find Dad's scrapbook of all the fires the department worked on. He'd keep clippings from the

Sacramento and L.A. papers, too, if they mentioned our area."

Evan slapped gray dust off his chinos and tan vest. "Where do you think it is?"

"Who knows? He used to keep the book at the station, but if it had been in the cabin…." She sighed as she recalled what the fire inspector reported after he finally came and went. No surprise he determined white gas was used as an accelerant. She'd returned to the site earlier this morning and found Max exploring the wet ashes and indiscernible black lumps. The purring cat seemed happy and unharmed.

Evan made a triumphant sound as he reached deep into a box and pulled out a stack of newsprint, still crisp and white. "Here, this should cover the last year."

"Thank you." Kitty quickly scanned the pages as Evan sat on a box next to her, so close the smell of spicy cologne and warm leather teased her nose. At one time, she would've been thrilled to be spending time with Evan, but today she couldn't get thoughts of Luke out of her head.

The last two nights she'd awakened from restless dreams and stared for hours at moonlight dancing over the beams above her head. She couldn't shake the image from the fire tower of Luke cupping her chin and gazing into her eyes. The connection between them sent additional alarms clanging through her head. In dangerous situations, people tended to bond quickly and emotions intensified. Emotions that could fade just as quickly, once life went back to normal.

She needed to be careful. Being with Luke's family and reuniting with acquaintances soothed an ache deep within, while at the same time raising questions about the choices she'd made. She prided herself on being independent, not relying on others to make her happy, but the feeling of something vital missing in her life persisted. Had she given up too much for her independence? Was loneliness or regret what drove her father to the church? Was he seeking a family? The thought stabbed her heart.

Luke and James had been through hard times and dealt with tragedy, but the family bond remained strong. They were good men, devoted to family, church and the community. Michael was obviously struggling with his loss. He needed a mother. Someone who could smooth out his rough edges and provide a snug home environment. Someone who didn't lack the skills she did with parenting and relationships. She rubbed her cheek. If only—

"Earth to Kitty." Evan waved his hand in front of her face.

She blinked. "Huh?"

"You've been staring at the same page for five minutes. What's with the goofy expression? You look like a lovesick puppy."

She punched him in the arm. "Are you calling me a dog?"

"Only if you stay on the floor like one. We could sit at my desk."

"Just a second." She leafed through the stack and held up a photo of a wildland fire from last fall. A wall of flames shot into the heavens below a mountain range she recognized. The fire burned about five miles from Pine Lake, but because of lack of wind, they easily contained it. "Did you take this photo?"

Evan glanced at the image. "Ew, no. Some freelance hack took those. I was out in Colorado."

Kitty rifled through the rest of the pages and winced at the headline: Town Loses Beloved Chief.

"This is what I'm looking for." She uncoiled her stiff legs and stood, then gathered the other articles she'd found on previous fires. "Can I make a copy of these older issues?"

"Thought you'd never ask. This way."

Kitty turned to go, but something caught her attention at the back door Evan had opened for cross-ventilation. "Hold on." She poked her head into the alley in time to see a flash of white go around the corner.

"What was it?" Evan asked, coming up behind her.

"Just a dog, I think. I didn't really see." She waved a finger at him. "And no jokes about me being with my own kind."

Evan snorted and guided her through another door to the main newspaper room, where an air conditioner hummed in a side window. He gestured to a machine in the corner. "I can't guarantee you'll get the cleanest copies, but it's all we got."

Kitty smiled at a sour-faced man slumped in a chair, feet on the smaller of two cluttered desks. "Hi, Franklin."

Franklin lifted the bill of his green baseball cap. "Oh, hey there, Miss Kitty. Nice to see you. Heard you were in town. If that machine gives you trouble, holler. All I do these days is fix things."

Kitty gazed around the spacious room with the high ceiling and spidery cracks in the plaster walls. "I still can't believe you bought this building," she remarked to Evan. "Being an ace reporter must have paid well."

"Let's just say I made some wise investments."

"Glad to hear it," Kitty said, remembering Evan's penchant for taking risks and gambling.

Evan looked over his shoulder at Franklin. "Aren't you supposed to be at lunch?"

"Yep, but Jerry went out to get me a part for the press and still hasn't returned." Franklin's chair creaked as he pulled his feet to the floor. "I don't understand this generation. All the kids do today is play video games or walk around with wires hanging from their ears."

The retired L.A. reporter slowly straightened with a hand

on his lower back. "You're going to need more toner for that gizmo. We have some in the storage closet."

He trudged to the rear of the building as Kitty placed the first article on the copier's glass and punched the button. The machine shuddered with the effort, but copies escaped out one end. "I never thought I'd see the day Pine Lake would have enough news to justify a weekly paper."

Evan laughed. "It doesn't really. We include a lot of state and world news to make up the difference." He perched on the edge of Franklin's desk and watched her with his inquisitive blue eyes. "Besides, it gives Franklin something productive to do everyday besides fish," he added loudly as the old man shuffled back into the room.

Franklin scowled. "You'd better watch it, you whipper-snapper. If I decide to retire full-time, who will you find willing to sit behind this rickety contraption you call a desk?" He slapped his hand on the surface, and the wood emitted an ominous creak.

Evan jumped to his feet. "What are you complaining about? You've been working on that desk for eight years. The new one is backordered. Another couple of weeks won't kill you."

"Like I haven't heard that before."

Kitty listened to the good-natured quarreling as she waited for the machine to crank out another copy. "By the way, Franklin, would you know of any more photographs of the Wildcat Ravine fire?"

Franklin stroked his gray beard. "Maybe. I did the layout on some of the articles. I think there's some in storage, but it'd be faster if you did an Internet search of California news-papers. My computer's got a great search engine that'll get you into what you want."

"That can wait," Evan said. "I don't want to hear belly-aching about it all afternoon if Sarah runs out of her noon special. I can run the search."

"If someone shows me how, I can do it," Kitty interjected. "I don't want to waste your time."

Evan glanced at Franklin who was firing up his desk computer. "Yeah, you can see how busy we are. Tell you what, you walk with Franklin over to the café, and I'll finish copying the articles for you and see what else I can find. You should eat. I'm worried about you."

"You are?"

He shouldered her away from the machine. "Yeah and hungry. You can bring me back something."

"Well, come to lunch then, and we can talk." Kitty said as Evan persistently guided her out the door to the porch.

"Nope, I'm still holding out for dinner, just the two of us, at my place. You free tonight?"

Kitty sighed. "I'm not sure. Depends on how the investigation is going. I'll call if I'm free. What can I get you at Sarah's?"

"A sandwich and a bottle of grape juice. By the time Franklin gets back, the juice will have turned to wine."

"I heard that," Franklin called.

Kitty smiled, glancing down Main Street. No sign of the Bronco. "If Luke arrives before I get back, can you send him over to the café?"

"Only if you insist. I'd rather keep you for myself the rest of the afternoon." He lowered his voice. "So, anything new to share?"

She shook her head. "Nothing you can use. Sorry." She and Luke had spent yesterday watching the fire video Ron shot from the tower, an excruciating experience as images of her father's last moments filled her head. Then they'd gone to the fire station and shifted through more of the scattered files, but they'd found nothing significant.

"Hey, can you order me a sandwich? Tuna on dark rye?" Franklin asked, joining them. "Jeremy was in the back alley while I was getting the toner, and he mentioned my new fishing reel came in. I'm going to go pick it up."

"I'll tell your boyfriend you're at the café," Evan called after her as she and Franklin trudged down the steps.

"He's not my boyfriend!" Kitty yelled back.

"Where've you been?" Sarah asked, smoothing her black skirt over her knee as she sat across the table from Kitty. "Now that's the cabin's gone, I want you to come stay in our guest room. I'm sure your Nana would feel better if you were staying with people who cared for you."

Kitty nearly choked on ice water. "You talked to Nana?"

"I was thinking of calling her this afternoon."

"Please don't tell her about the cabin. She'll fret and make herself sick. The chief and I are trying to wrap up Dad's case as quickly as possible. But if this goes on much longer, I'll consider coming over."

Sarah pursed her lips until after Clarence served Kitty a turkey burger garnished with avocado and Ortega chili and a side of crispy seasoned fries. "So, you'll still be here for the festival? The theme is the Wild West this year."

"I thought that was the theme every year."

Sarah tapped her polished fingernail on the red tablecloth. "I have the perfect costume for you. A darling designer original. Midnight blue, which will bring out the sapphire in your eyes."

"I don't know, Sarah—"

"Nonsense. Under the circumstances you deserve to have fun."

"Okay, I'll see," she hedged. If she wasn't home by next

week, she'd have to take unpaid leave. Kitty bit into the burger and sighed. How she'd missed Sarah's turkey burgers.

"What have you got there?" Sarah pointed to the paper at Kitty's elbow.

"A copy of a *Tribune* article on the Wildcat fire."

Sarah sighed. "Kitty, I think I can speak for your father since we were such close friends. He'd want to you to stop trying to fix the past and get on with your life."

"I wish I could stop, Sarah, but I can't until I clear his name."

Sarah frowned. "You're just as pigheaded as he was. He'd get an idea in his head and just wouldn't let go. Sometimes things just happen. Fate isn't always kind or fair." She glanced around her. "For example, what's fair about me ending up in a dump like this?"

Kitty's mouth dropped open. "I thought you loved it here."

Sarah shook her head. "Now see? Things aren't always as they appear. Everyone has secrets, hidden desires—unspoken dreams—including your father." The bell on the door jingled. Sarah rose and waved a couple to a nearby table. She handed them menus, took their drink order and marched stoically off to the kitchen.

Kitty choked down the rest of her lunch and pondered the bitter edge in Sarah's tone. She had no idea Sarah wasn't satisfied with her café and nice home. Had her father been unhappy about the way his life had turned out too?

When Sarah finally returned, the familiar, mischievous sparkle was back in her eyes, which usually meant she had some juicy gossip to share. "Did I tell you about Pete and Jane Miller—"

A whooshing sound cut off her words, followed by a deafening blast. The café shook as if in the epicenter of an earthquake. Kitty grabbed the table edge as her plate clattered to the floor. An instant later, everything went deathly still, except for the rattling pots in the kitchen.

Kitty stared wide-eyed at Sarah, and they bolted through the door to the sidewalk with the other occupants. People ran frantically past them up the street, and she raced along with them.

Smoke poured out of the *Tribune* building's shattered windows. The wall of the storage room where she and Evan had searched the boxes was blown out. Flames hungrily licked the edges of the hole, taunting the fire station siren echoing throughout the valley.

Shock and horror gripped her as she shoved her way to the front of the building. Someone charging along the sidewalk slammed into her, nearly knocking her down. She stared at the open door and windows.

Was Evan still inside? And where was Luke? He'd planned to meet her at the newspaper office. She started up the steps, glass crunching under her boots. A shout went up from the gathering crowd. Evan backed out the front door, dragging a motionless body. She stifled a scream in her throat. He stumbled and she leapt forward to support him. Others rushed to carry the man to the sidewalk. Kitty's heart pounded as they turned him over.

Franklin.

"Evan, is anyone else in the building?" she shouted above the wail of the approaching fire trucks. *Oh, please, God, if you're listening, let Luke be okay. Pastor James said all I had to do was ask, and I'm begging. Please.*

Evan stared dazedly at her from his position on the ground. Kitty tugged on his sleeve. "Evan, is anyone else is in the office? The office boy? What was his name? Jerry! Was he in there? And did Luke come looking for me?"

His eyes focused on hers, and he shook his head. Another small explosion erupted, and hot air blasted her face. Kitty fought the urge to charge inside to check for herself. Even if she tried, the heat would sear her lungs in seconds if she went in without protection.

Focus on what you can do. She placed her hand on Franklin's ribs. Had he stopped breathing? Quickly, she straightened Franklin's head to open his airway and placed her cheek close to his lips to feel for air as she felt along his neck for a pulse. There was neither, and Kitty launched into the CPR breathing routine and rhythm that had become second nature to her.

"One, two, three…" She counted out loud as she pushed on his sternum after giving him two breaths. She could vaguely hear people shouting and running. What if Evan was wrong and Luke lay in the burning building, dying? She shoved the thought away and concentrated on Franklin.

"Kitty!" someone called, and she glanced up to see Jeremy pushing through the crowd.

"Switch to two-person CPR on your count," he said, kneeling next to her. Kitty nodded gratefully. The concrete was grinding into her knees, and she needed to shift her weight.

"Switch on the next breath." Kitty pushed harder on Franklin's chest. "Twelve, thirteen, fourteen, fifteen." She stopped the chest compressions as Jeremy squeezed air into Franklin's lungs with a blue Ambu bag he'd fitted over the patient's mouth. Kitty felt again for a pulse on Franklin's neck, and shook her head at Jeremy as they switched places.

"Come on, Franklin, breathe. You want to try out your new fishing reel, don't you?" she said over the panic clogging her throat. The fire engines had arrived, and Daniel shouted commands. Evan lay on a medic backboard as several firefighters worked around him.

"Jeremy, did you see the chief?" she asked.

"Nope," he said between counts of compressions. A crash

reverberated from inside the building and sparks flew toward the cloudless sky. Her stomach churned, and for the first time in her career, terror gripped her on scene.

"A helicopter's on the way," Luke's voice shouted in the distance.

She looked over her shoulder at his grim face and nearly collapsed with relief.

Thank You, God!

"We're clearing a landing place on the beach." Luke strode away tossing about commands to his men like a warrior throwing spears. Kitty's body sagged from spent adrenaline, and her fingers trembled as she squeezed the bag.

Jeremy tired, and they switched places again. After what seemed an eternity, the emergency helicopter's beating blades drowned out everything else. The paramedics surged from the chopper, hooked a monitor on Franklin and loaded him into the helicopter. She knew they'd continue CPR until a doctor declared him dead or otherwise. She bowed her head. *Please, God don't let him die.*

Jeremy gently nudged her with his elbow, and they trudged to the beach to watch the helicopter take off. She scanned the crowd for Luke, but once again, he'd disappeared.

She smiled wearily at Jeremy. "You were great back there."

"Yeah, I was, wasn't I?" Jeremy pulled out a cigarette pack, his fingers shaking, and offered one to Kitty.

She shook her head. "Those things will kill you."

"Not if something else gets me first," he said. "I'll fill out the medical report, and you can check it over later." He slipped away as Luke strolled toward them, his expression impassive.

"I need to talk to you." He grabbed Kitty's hand and pulled her across the street until they stood alone in the alley beside the café. He unstrapped his helmet and tossed it aside. His chest beneath his turnout coat heaved with deep breaths.

"What happened?" Fear rocked her. "Did Franklin die?"

Luke shook his head and backed her toward the wall, his arms on either side of her. His dark eyes, now full of pain, gazed into hers. "I thought I'd lost you."

She nodded. "And I thought I'd lost—"

His lips covered hers, the tender kiss drowning her words. Waves of sweet acceptance rolled over her as she kissed him back. A car honked on the street. Luke lifted his head, his arms wrapping her in an embrace. Kitty leaned against him, her face pressed against the rough fabric of his jacket. She'd never felt so right, so at home with anyone.

"We're in trouble," she barely heard him say above the thudding of her heart.

"I know," Kitty whispered.

TEN

Luke walked out on his deck to where Kitty stared at the distant blackened shell of the *Tribune* building. The department had swiftly put the fire out, but smoke still drifted hazily against the Four Sisters.

"Just heard from the gas company. Apparently someone opened the heater valve in the back room at the *Tribune,* and gas caused the explosion," he said.

"Intentionally or accidentally?"

"That's the big question. Evan says he has no clue, and Franklin is in no condition to speak yet."

Kitty's eyes glistened. "I feel like this is my fault. If I hadn't gone there—"

"Stop. No matter how this happened it is not your fault. Good news is that Evan just has some scratches and smoke inhalation. They'll probably release him from the hospital tomorrow morning." Luke smoothed her soft, unruly hair from her shoulders. He yearned to kiss her like he had in the alley, but he didn't dare test the implications of that desire yet. "You've been through a lot. I can't promise you everything will ever be all right, but in time it'll get easier."

"How do you know?" She nestled close to him.

He shuddered inwardly, reliving the agony from when he thought she was trapped in Stone's burning building. "You're feeling hurt and betrayed because death is so final. There are no second chances. No chances to fix what went wrong."

She tilted her head to look up at him. "Is that what happened with Michael's mother?"

Luke sighed, the familiar knife of self-recrimination twisting in his gut. "Not many people know, but a little over a year ago, Michael was kidnapped. It took nine months to find him and it about killed me. But I got through it. My wife didn't. Miranda lost her faith in God and me. She started drinking. One night she got in the car and..."

"Oh, Luke, I'm so sorry. How horrible."

He swallowed the lump in his throat. "I got Michael back, and I thank God every day that he wasn't physically abused. People think I'm overprotective. Rationally, I know chances of something like this happening again are slim, but emotionally Michael and I aren't there yet."

"Perfectly understandable." Kitty said, her eyes glistening. "It takes time."

Luke sighed, longing to tell her everything, but caution held his tongue. The less people knew he was ex-FBI, the less likely someone else from his past, like Sorensen, might seek vengeance.

"I never told Michael how his mother died. He has enough to deal with. But somehow he must've found out, judging from the questions about being drunk that he asked you the other night." He shuddered at what Sorenson might have told Michael. "I'm sure he blames me. Sometimes he looks at me with such anger."

"Best thing would be to sit down and talk to him about it," James said from behind them.

Luke turned. "Dad. I didn't know you were here."

"Just got in," he said, his face lined with fatigue. "I went to the hospital and prayed with Franklin's wife. He's still unconscious. I can't do anything more for him right now, but you, my boy, can set things right with your son. You need to tell Michael the truth about his mother."

"What if I'm wrong and he doesn't know? The counselor said to wait until he's older."

Kitty moved discreetly away as James put a hand on Luke's shoulder. "You can't protect him from the past forever. Pray about it. When the time is right, God will let you know what to do."

"I didn't do nothing wrong," Michael shouted from the living room.

"Now what?" Luke groaned and strode inside. "Michael, stop yelling. What happened?"

Elizabeth set a large picnic basket on table. "Michael ran away from Mrs. Johnson's house today. Again."

"What's this, Michael?" Luke's voice thundered before he got it under control. Jack whined, looking from Michael to Luke.

Michael kicked the rug. "I just took a walk. What's the big deal? I told you it was boring over there. I don't need a babysitter. I want to go back to Chicago. I hate you, and I hate it here!" He ran from the room, Jack on his heels.

"Oh, Michael," Luke whispered hoarsley.

"I'm sorry. I should've waited to tell you privately." Elizabeth's lips trembled. "He's just so angry."

James shook his head. "You didn't do anything wrong. Michael has to deal with the consequences of his actions."

"I don't suppose anyone is hungry now, but I brought some fried chicken." Elizabeth lifted the checkered towel covering the basket.

"You're such a blessing," James said, rubbing his hands together. "Comfort food, just what the doctor ordered. It's been a hard day, and I think we'll all feel better if we eat something. We'll take Michael something when he calms down some."

"Yes, thank you for the food, Elizabeth." Luke pulled a chair out for Kitty. He went through the motions of eating, although everything was tasteless to him. His dad kept the conversation flowing with Elizabeth and Kitty, discussing church activities and the upcoming festival. Kitty shot Luke a few concerned looks, but she didn't speak directly to him until James and Elizabeth were in the kitchen putting the leftovers away.

"Would it be all right if I took a plate to Michael?" Kitty reached under the table and squeezed Luke's hand. "I'd like to talk to him. I think I can relate some to what he's going through. Don't worry—I won't discuss anything concerning his mother that you haven't already."

Luke sighed. "You can't do any worse than I do. Go ahead. Just don't expect a civilized conversation." Luke stood to finish clearing the table as Kitty quickly assembled a plateful of chicken and potato salad and headed for the stairs.

"I have some notes I need to add to my sermon," his father said, emerging from the kitchen. "Thank you for dinner, Elizabeth. Perhaps I'll see you tomorrow. I'll be helping to set up the church booth for the festival."

"I'm looking forward to it," Elizabeth said to James before he ambled away. She smiled at Luke. "Well, it's just the two of us now, but I should be going soon too." She set her picnic basket on the table and gathered up her red-checkered towels and napkins.

Luke cleared his throat, his father's advice about the truth lingering in his head. "There is something I need to say. You've been a great friend to all of us, but—"

"Oh, I enjoy being here. I miss having family around…and I love being able to take care of you all," she said, slipping on her pink sweater. "It's no trouble."

He cleared his throat again. "It's not that—"

"Wait." Elizabeth laid her hand gently on his arm. "It's

okay. I should've known I couldn't hide my feelings. You've guessed, haven't you?"

"Well I—"

"I'd never try to take your mother's place, but your father and I love each other. I hope you understand and don't make this hard for him."

What? Luke's knees nearly gave out, and he sank down on a chair. "B-but you're young enough to be his daughter."

Elizabeth tsked. "How flattering, but I'm not that young. I have good genes," she said, pulling the strap of her purse over her shoulder. "Now, I really do need to go. I'm still getting my crafts ready to display at the festival. I'll see you tomorrow."

The door closed and he sat frozen, his head buried in hands. His father and Elizabeth? Here he'd thought his dad liked the elderly librarian. But this made sense now that he thought back to the many times he'd come across his father and Elizabeth together, the smiles they exchanged and how his Dad raved about her cooking.

The kiss he'd shared with Kitty flashed across his brain. He could hardly bear to think of his Dad and Elizabeth doing the same.

He lifted his head, running his fingers through his hair. All this time he thought she was making a play for him. How blind could he be? One thing for sure, he'd never understand women.

Kitty lingered on the stairway, plotting her strategy. She had no experience with ten-year-old boys, especially those carrying such emotional baggage. What she'd learned from Luke made her own childhood angst seem like a trip to Disneyland by comparison.

She knocked. "Michael, it's Kitty. Can I come in? I brought you some dinner."

"I'm not supposed to eat up here."

She smiled. "Since when would that stop you? Besides, your dad said it was okay."

The door opened slowly and Jack growled. "It's okay." Michael told the dog, and Jack let Kitty sidle past them.

Built under the eaves of the house, the room glowed with cedar. Skylights, spaced evenly among the beams, showcased the stars. A glass-paneled wall provided a spectacular view of the lake and town below. Bright southwestern rugs adorned the hardwood floor.

"I love your room, Michael," she said, handing him the plate. "Where's your bed?"

"Over there in the fort." He pointed to a wall section housing a maze of smooth-as-silk varnished wood that created passageways and chambers just the right size for a boy to explore.

"The wall opens up like this." He pushed on a panel and the front section slid sideways revealing bunk beds. "My dad and grandpa made it. They're planning to open a carpentry business. Maybe we'll be rich someday."

"Well, you're so lucky. I would have loved to have a room like this." Kitty flopped beside him on the shaggy rug while Michael devoured his chicken dinner, dripping honey-mustard sauce on his blue striped shirt. She patted Jack, and his thick, white-tipped tail thumped on the floor.

Kitty lay on her back and gazed through the skylight at the twinkling stars in the clear sky. "You saw the *Tribune* Building blow up, didn't you? I didn't realize at the time, but I saw you and Jack in the alley while I was searching for newspaper articles. I saw Jack's white tail go around the corner."

Michael's drumstick dropped to the floor. "Huh?" he asked, his facial features freezing, so much like his father's when he tried to conceal emotion.

She turned on her side, propping her head on her hand. "You may be the only one who saw everything. Must've been cool to see the building explode."

Michael scrunched up his mouth as if ready to protest further, but then he shrugged with a sheepish grin. "The windows and doors blew out just like in the movies. It *was* pretty cool. How come it exploded?"

"They think the gas was left on. It smells like rotten eggs, but apparently no one noticed."

"Yeah, it smelled gross."

"What?" Kitty asked, her stomach turning over. She sat up. "You were actually in the building?"

Michael scooted backward a few feet. "Promise you won't tell my dad? I'll run away if you tell."

She gasped. "I can't promise something like that." Luke needed to know, but what if Michael did run away and something happened to him? It would kill Luke. She chewed on her lower lip. "Here's the deal. I'll give you a day to tell your father you were there, and if you can't or won't, I'll do it."

"Why?" He drew his legs up and wrapped his arms around his knees.

"Because you might've seen something that could help the sheriff." His scowl deepened, so she added brightly, "You could help solve the case. You'd be a hero."

He rested his chin on his knees as he stared at her. "Like a detective on TV?"

"Yeah, like Colombo."

"Who?"

Kitty sighed. "Never mind. Now, try to remember. Did you see who was in the newspaper office?"

"Mr. Stone was there. I saw him get a drink of water, and the old man with the funny beard was sort of yelling at him."

"Where were you?"

"In that room with all the boxes. I made a secret fort. Then I thought I heard someone coming, and I ran away."

"You mean like Mr. Stone or the old man?"

"No, I don't think so. Someone else was already in the back, and then it smelled bad." His gaze shifted to his shoes, and he blinked hard. "The old man is going to die, isn't he?"

Kitty sucked in a painful breath. "We don't know yet. Franklin was hurt pretty badly."

"My mom died."

"I'm sorry. I know it's hard. My mother didn't die, but she left when I was about your age. I haven't seen her since."

"Why?"

"I don't know. Maybe she thought I'd have a better life here in Pine Lake, like what your father wants for you."

"Why did it take him so long to find me?" Michael asked with a catch in his voice. He buried his head in arms.

Kitty placed her hands on Michael's cheeks and tilted his face so she could look him in the eyes. "I have no doubt your father moved heaven and earth to find you. If he couldn't get to you sooner, it wasn't his fault. He never ever gave up. Don't ever forget that."

Michael squeezed his eyes shut and nodded.

Kitty stood, stretching her cramped legs. "Now, remember, talk to your father about being at the *Tribune* or I'll have to. It's the right thing to do, and you'll both feel better."

She closed his door. Poor kid. Being ripped away from his family and losing his mother punched a hole in his heart that would never completely heal. Luke needed to find a way to soothe the ache and help Michael learn to cope before he emotionally withdrew from the world.

Like she had.

"What's this?" Michael muffled voice came from the back of Kitty's Jeep, parked beside the open bay doors to the fire station. He held up two yellow bundles.

"Fire shelters," Kitty answered. "And, no, you can't open them. They're for emergencies." She sighed and slipped off her sunglasses, placing them on the dash. It had been three days since Michael informed Kitty that he'd talked to his father about being at the *Tribune* building. Just like they'd agreed. Because Luke hadn't brought it up, she decided to not interfere and let them work it out on their own. Over time, their moods seemed to lighten while her's grew heavier.

She and Luke hadn't made any further progress in the investigation. No new evidence had been uncovered. Franklin still lay unconscious in intensive care. Kitty remained perplexed about her relationship with Luke. Sometimes Luke's hand brushed hers while they watched the fire video again or pored over reports. Occasionally, she thought she detected a longing in his eyes, but there had been no more kisses. Kitty surmised the bewildering emotions that overwhelmed her shook him as well. He had to deal with the memories of his late wife and consider what was best for his son. Whereas she was torn between two worlds—her life in L.A. and the one here that'd sprung to life with an earth-shattering kiss in an alley.

Last night she began a Bible study, trying to connect to whatever interested her father in those last days. For Sam to go searching for God, he had to have a strong reason. Pastor James eagerly supplied her with a series designed for young adults. So far, she'd found the first two lessons interesting and was amazed at what she remembered from her younger, churchgoing years.

Today, she was just glad to leave the house. Luke insisted on caution, and she'd stayed out of sight over the last couple days. The shootings in the ravine and *Tribune* explosion spurred a flurry of activity and rumors. Kitty had even offered to move to another location to make things easier for the Tanner family, but Luke insisted it was too late. Whatever trouble plagued her engulfed them as well. They were more secure sticking together, watching each other's backs.

"What are the shelters for?" Michael asked, interrupting her thoughts.

"They're like a tent in case you get caught in a firestorm you can't outrun. You crawl inside, and the fire won't burn you." *In theory.*

"Wow! Have you ever been caught in a fire?"

"No. I've never had to use a fire shelter." *Thank you, God.*

"Bummer." His voice dripped with disappointment. "You sure have a lot of junk back here."

"Yeah, well, you never know if you're going to need something," Kitty said, bumping noses with Jack, who'd claimed the passenger seat.

"Is this gold?" Michael held up her father's specimen of pyrite that must've fallen out of her pocket.

"No, it's pyrite, fool's gold."

"Too bad."

"I agree."

Michael dropped the rock back on the floor and reached under the seat. He popped up again, this time with a small, spiral-bound notebook in his hand. "What's this for?"

"That's my mileage log. Put it back, please. I—" She stared at the notebook as every nerve in her body seemed to come alert. "Oh, Michael, I could kiss you."

He scrunched up his face. "Gross."

"What's gross?" Luke strode up, breathtakingly handsome in his blue uniform shirt and black jeans.

Kitty's heart fluttered. "Kisses,"

"Not with the right person, they're not." Luke's gaze met Kitty's and her pulse raced. "So what's worth a kiss?"

"Huh? Oh!" Kitty grinned. "Michael reminded me of

something. I think my father's missing notebook is in the Bronco."

Luke shook his head. "Sorry to disappoint you, but I've cleaned the cab out several times. The sheriff also went through it."

"There's a place along the headliner where the fabric's unraveled at the seam. You wouldn't even notice it unless you knew it was there." She dashed over to the Bronco, excitement mounting as she felt along to the ribbed ceiling seam near the door. With a cry of delight, she pulled out a small memo notebook from deep within the foam that insulated the cab.

"Can I see?" Michael yelled.

"Maybe, in a little while." She clutched the book tightly, suddenly afraid to read the contents. The answers to why her father went to Wildcat Ravine could be in there. Once she'd found out the truth about her father, she'd be free of Pine Lake. She glanced at Luke who grinned, sharing her excitement, and cold doubt shot through her.

Would the price of freedom cost more than she'd bargained for?

ELEVEN

Luke leaned over the table, his head inches from Kitty, trying to focus on Sam's notebook as she flipped through the pages. They'd delivered Michael to his grandfather and convened at Sarah's Café so they could concentrate on work. However, the wildflower scent emanating from Kitty's hair, the soft smoothness of her arm pressed against his and the proximity of her pink lips sent his senses into overdrive. He was both irritated and thankful Sheriff Johnson sat across from them, watching them with his beady, ice-blue eyes.

"The log ends on June fifteenth," Kitty said, disappointment in her voice. "He must've started another book."

"Let me see." Luke reached for the notebook and examined it carefully. "No, look. The pages were torn out. The last third of the notebook is missing."

"Why would someone rip out pages? Why wouldn't they destroy the whole thing instead?" Johnson asked, forking up Sarah's meatloaf. "Makes no sense to me."

"Sam must've done it." Luke opened to the last page with handwriting on it. "It shows he went down to the county agency in the morning but came back by noon. And over here, he wrote 3:00 and L.F. Do you recognize those initials?"

"I—" Kitty's throat went dry as he flipped to the back cover.

Call Kitty was written on the flap. "He never called, but...." Her fingers twisted the napkin in her lap, her knuckles white.

"Are you okay?" he asked, wishing he could hold her close and offer comfort. He'd purposely kept an emotional and physical distance between them the last couple days to give them both time to pause and think before feelings over-ruled common sense. With Michaels well-being at stake, he couldn't afford to make a mistake.

Kitty nodded, keeping her gaze on the notebook.

He glanced at Johnson. "Anything new on the *Tribune* fire?"

Swallowing, Johnson lifted his napkin and carefully wiped his mouth. "Not anything the county fire investigation team didn't find. Gas leak from the heater. The main valve's in the utility closet. Could've been an accident. The valve reportedly was loose. Someone could've knocked into it, although Stone says no one on his staff had been in the closet recently."

Kitty looked up. "But Michael said he'd heard someone in the closet."

"He said what?" Luke's voice rose. "Michael was in the building?"

Kitty's face paled. "Why, yes. He said he told you."

Fear and betrayal slammed into him, constricting his lungs. He thought he could trust this woman. His son had been in mortal danger, and she hadn't thought it important enough to mention it until now?

Kitty shifted away from him. "I thought he told you days ago. I made a deal with him. You both seemed to be getting along so well...."

He gritted his teeth with frustration. "He's a child, Kitty. A child who has a history of lying, and it didn't occur to you to check with me if he'd followed through?"

Two spots flamed red on her cheeks. "Yes it did, but I

thought it'd be good for someone to trust him. To give him a chance to do the right thing. I just assumed… I'm sorry."

"Michael never mentioned the *Tribune*. He told me he'd climbed out the window, and he promised not to do it again. We talked about his mother too, but that was all." At the time, Michael's attempt to reconcile appeared heartfelt, giving Luke hope they'd finally taken a step forward. He'd actually credited Kitty for the positive change he'd seen. In reality, his child had confided in a relative stranger and treated his own father like a fool.

The sheriff cleared his throat. "Apparently, we have a communication problem. Luke, I'll need to talk to Michael."

"Apparently so do I," Luke said, fighting to remain calm and in his seat. Every nerve in his body screamed for action. Only it was too late. Once again, Luke hadn't been there to protect Michael. He shifted his narrowed gaze to Kitty. "What else did my son say?"

She gnawed on her lower lip. "He said he was in the back of the building before the explosion. He thought he heard someone else, too."

"Any chance the kid turned on the gas himself? By accident?" Johnson asked.

"He wasn't in the right place," Kitty said as Sarah snatched up Kitty's barely touched plate and sniffed it.

"Something wrong with the food?"

"Sorry, Sarah." Kitty patted her arm. "I'm just not hungry. Your meat loaf is delicious, though."

"Now, don't you go trying to butter me up." Sarah shifted her gaze to the notebook on the table. Luke flipped the cover shut and shoved the book to the sheriff.

"We're finished here." Luke pushed back his chair as the sheriff did the same. "Put it on my tab." He followed Johnson out to the porch while Kitty lingered in the café to speak with Sarah.

"Sam logged in a lot of miles." The sheriff loosened his belt and smothered a belch.

"Perhaps he suspected someone from the beginning and was in the process of investigating."

"The fires stopped after his death until about a month ago. Before the incidences at the campground and Sam's cabin, I figured the recent fires and burglaries were random occurrences. Now, I'm not so sure." He slid a glance at Luke before tipping his hat to some passing ladies. "Any word from your contact at the bureau?"

"Alec is still following money trails and doing background checks on everyone Sam was associated with. Alec's good, but like I said, these things take time."

The door jingled and Kitty bounded out of the café. "I know what the initials L.F. stand for. He went to see Nathaniel Ferguson."

"Then shouldn't the initials be N.F.?" the sheriff asked.

Kitty shrugged. "I don't know why, but Dad nicknamed him Lucky, so the initials would be L.F."

"So, we need to find Lucky." Luke said, avoiding Kitty's gaze. He knew he had probably hurt her, but now wasn't the time to discuss it.

A dirt-covered SUV roared to a stop in front of the diner. Jeremy Wright unfolded his long legs from the interior. He caught sight of Luke and scowled. Luke sighed. He didn't have the energy to deal with the disgruntled firefighter right now. He had enough problems.

"Nathaniel won the lottery a couple years ago and gave the million to research for children's cancer. His only son died from leukemia." Johnson said to Luke, stepping aside as Jeremy stomped up the steps.

"It was on national news a couple years ago," Kitty added.

"I don't recall the story," he said, suppressing a shudder. Two years ago, Luke was totally consumed in finding Michael.

"He's a biologist and roams the outback most of the year working on research projects," Johnson said. "There's a hiker's shelter on Black Sheep's pass he uses quite frequently. I can send a deputy up. If Nathaniel's not there, he can leave a message. I'll call the forestry service, and ask the rangers to keep an eye out for him too."

"The fewer people who know we're looking for him the better," Luke said as his radio vibrated and then squawked. A moment later, the fire station siren blew across the valley, sending them running for their vehicles.

"What is it?" Kitty asked, jumping into the cab and slamming the truck door shut.

Luke turned up the volume of the radio. "Fire. Southwest of town and moving fast."

"Here's a pager. If we need backup, I'll let you know," Luke said, his voice cool and detached. He paused in the doorway of his house. "I'll head out with the second shift wildland fire crew and relieve Daniel."

"I want to go with you now," Kitty said, although she knew it was futile. Luke had insisted she stay in town. After they'd checked in at the fire station, she'd retrieved her Jeep, and followed him home.

"Here's how you operate the alarm box." He made her do a trial run-through with the number set and handed her a card with the code. "Don't go anywhere alone or take chances. My father is at the church with Michael, but he can come home if you need anything. I wouldn't leave, but we're short on men. I'll be back as soon as I can." He turned and strode down the steps.

She followed. "Luke, I'm sorry about Michael. It won't happen again."

"No, it won't." He climbed into the Bronco without a backward glance and took off, the hot, steady wind whisking dust into the sky. Kitty sighed as a hollow sensation grew in her chest. Luke had been carefully polite since finding out about Michael's near miss, but the wall between them had grown thicker. She couldn't blame him. His biggest fear was that something would happen to Michael again. She got chills thinking about Michael being in the *Tribune* building.

Kitty closed the door and obediently set the alarm. Who was she kidding? She didn't fit in here. She didn't fit in anywhere, except at work. But at least in the city there were others like her, secure in anonymity. Luke was a good, God-fearing man with a traumatic past and a damaged child. He didn't need someone else in his life with a risky job and seemingly always in the middle of trouble. Luke needed a wife who delighted in cooking and housekeeping, and had the right instincts to raise kids. Someone like Jordan wanted. Someone she was not.

Heartsick with regret, she packed her bag and threw it in the Jeep. She'd explain to Sarah what was going on and see if her offer of a room was still open. It would be better for everyone. Somehow she'd just have to make Sarah promise not to call Nana.

She fired up her Jeep, but the closer she got to town, the uneasier she became. Had she made the right decision? Suddenly, an urge to confer with Pastor James filled her, and she veered off to the church.

Michael lounged on the front steps with a bored expression. When he spied the Jeep, he jumped to his feet and started to take off.

"Michael! Where do you think you're going?" Kitty slammed the door shut and strode up the sidewalk.

He glared at her, arms folded over his chest. "You're trying to take him away."

"Who are you talking about? Your father?" Kitty stopped at the bottom of the concrete steps. "That's ridiculous."

"You snitched on me."

"Yeah. So? You lied to me. I looked like an idiot."

"He's mad at me, and it's all your fault. I wish you'd never come here. Just go away." He turned and ran into the church, darting around his grandfather in the foyer.

Pastor James stepped out on the landing and gave her a kind smile. "It's not your fault. He's confused and trying to sort out his feelings."

Kitty leaned on the metal railing. "My presence here isn't helping."

"Nonsense. He'll be fine. You just have to leave everything in God's hands. Have faith. You've made progress over the last week. I'd hate to see this slow you down."

"I won't stop the Bible studies. I think I have an idea of what my dad was seeking, and I'll keep searching the scripture. I just wish I didn't feel like I failed my father." And everyone else. She blinked back burning tears. "Maybe it sounds cowardly, but I don't want to risk failing someone else. You can tell Michael that he doesn't have to worry. I have no intention of stealing his father or settling down in Pine Lake ever again."

"Welcome to my humble abode," Evan said, unlocking the door to his lakeside cottage. He walked with a limp and a large bandage decorated his forehead, but no one would've guessed the man had been blown out of a building only days before.

"This isn't so humble. I've always admired this place. Lucky you." Kitty smiled. Evan had found her talking in the café with Sarah and managed to convince her to visit. Longing to be working the fire instead of waiting around, she needed a distraction. After depositing her belongings in Sarah's spare room, she followed Evan home.

"Excuse the mess," Evan said as Kitty entered. Not only were the walls covered with framed photographs, but large prints leaned against the walls and stood stacked on every surface.

"Come in the dining area and have a seat. My new stuff's in there."

She paused beside a row of black-and-white scenes that looked to be set in the Far East. Poorly clad children and mothers with haunting despair in their eyes picked through the ruins of their homes as tanks drove past in massive dust clouds. "Weren't these published in *Time* magazine?"

"Yep," Evan answered from the kitchen. "Do you want coffee? Tea? Lemonade?"

"I'll take a glass of water, thanks." Kitty abandoned the war pictures and wandered to the table that supported more wildlife pictures. She sorted through them until Evan appeared with ice water and a pretzel bag.

She held up some shots of a bear and her cubs frolicking in a stream. "These are wonderful."

"Yes, aren't they?" Evan grinned. "I have a show scheduled in Los Angeles next month. I was hoping we'd get together in the city." He stood framed in the large bay window, and the lake water glittered so brightly, spots danced in front of Kitty's eyes. She blinked. Next month? She'd avoided thinking that far ahead.

"Sounds fun." She shifted her feet and hit something under the table. Ducking, she saw she'd kicked over a box.

"Oh, don't worry about those." He squatted to help Kitty shove photos back.

She lifted a color shot of a deer and a fawn fleeing a wall of flames. "What fire was this?"

Evan took the photograph from her and studied it. "Not

sure. I'd have to check on the computer." He tossed it under the table.

Kitty leaned back in the chair. "Speaking of fires, have you learned any more about the explosion in your building?"

Evan's index finger traced the bandage on his forehead. "I have my own theory, but at this point, it doesn't matter. Insurance will cover it. Let's not discuss anything so unpleasant on this beautiful day. What I want is your opinion on which of these I should use for my upcoming L.A. exhibition." He retrieved a hefty portfolio file. "Tell me what visually intrigues you and what moves you emotionally."

Kitty poured over the photographs with Evan for an hour. When they'd finished to Evan's satisfaction, he asked, "How about dinner? I have some steaks in the freezer that we could barbecue on the deck."

She fiddled with her pager and glanced at her watch. Nearly four o'clock, and Luke still hadn't called her. "The steaks sound great, but I better get back. I'm supposed to be helping Sarah with the festival booth."

"We have time. They postponed the festival opening until tomorrow night because of the fire danger." He took her hand and rubbed it between his. "Please stay—I want to talk about us."

"Us?"

"With the newspaper gone, I'm thinking of starting over and making Los Angeles my home base."

Kitty stared at him. Even with a bruised face and stitches holding his eyebrow together, he exuded a boyish charm. At one time she might've thought them suitably matched in terms of their lifestyles. They enjoyed independence, adventure and living on the edge without any real personal commitments. Evan couldn't care less if she cooked or cleaned house. And she knew he didn't want children. Sounded ideal except…after being in the proximity of Luke's family for a short time, that carefree way of life lacked luster now.

"Oh, Evan." Kitty gently pulled her hand from his grasp. "We're just good buddies who share a past."

"I always thought you wanted more from me."

Kitty swept her bangs from her forehead. "A weak moment when I was fifteen. I blame it on hormones."

"What about now?" Evan captured both her hands this time. "We're not teenagers, and I'm very interested in more." He kissed one of her fingertips, then another. "Very interested, indeed."

Laughter exploded from her lips. "I'm sorry." She sputtered. "It's just I heard you giving the same line to Susie Morrey behind the gym in high school. It's your standard operating procedure."

Evan grinned and shrugged. "And it usually works." He leaned closer. "Don't be fooled by my lack of originality. We'd be great together, Kitcat. We're cast from the same mold. Can't you feel the energy between us?"

"Oh, is that what this is?" Kitty said teasingly, but Evan's expression remained serious. She didn't want to hurt him so she fumbled for the right words. "Evan, I appreciate how you feel, but I'm a poor bet when it comes to romantic relationships. Let's not ruin the friendship we have."

Evan studied her face and then a cocky smile flashed. "It's Tanner, isn't it?"

Kitty's face flushed. "What do you mean?"

"Sarah said you've been staying at Tanner's house. It is easy to deduce what's going on."

"I don't like what you're implying. Yes I stayed there, but with Luke's father and son, too." Kitty stood, ready to leave, but was distracted by the view of a sailboat flying by on the lake. The wind was strengthening. She glanced at her pager again. Why hadn't Luke called? Surely they needed help by now.

"If I were you, I wouldn't get too attached to Tanner. He's a loser." His confident smirk angered her.

"Just mind your own business, Evan. I need to go." She marched to the front door, but Evan caught up with her, pulling her into his arms.

"Kitty, be reasonable. I know you care about me."

She was lifting her hands to shove him away when a cough sounded behind them.

"Tanner. Don't you know how to knock?" Evan glanced over his shoulder, giving Kitty a chance to jerk away from his grip.

Luke gazed at Kitty, emotions masked, but his stance radiated anger. "Kitty, let's go."

"She doesn't have to leave just because you say so." Evan smirked, his body blocking the door.

"She does if she wants to keep working for me."

"You should be so lucky."

"Enough!" Kitty said, shoving past both men to the porch. "Evan, thank you for showing me your photos. Luke, this better be important." She spun and marched to her Jeep, blowing out an exasperated breath when Luke joined her. "You could've just paged me."

He glanced back at Evan, still watching from his doorway. "I thought you were going to wait for me at the house. I was worried."

Her heart quickened, but she steeled herself against the concern in voice. "You said not go anywhere *alone*. I was with Evan, and I've arranged to stay with Sarah. I think distance will be better for all of us. Safer." She yanked open the Jeep door and then paused. "Why are you back early? What's going on with the fire?"

He remained silent for a few painful moments, his

expression lost in the darkness. "Forestry took over. The fire should be contained in the canyon by morning, but it burned the shelter in the pass."

Kitty's stomach clenched. "And Lucky?"

"Don't know yet. He should've been able to escape. But there's something else I need to tell you." he said in a somber tone that filled her with cold apprehension.

"I'm afraid to ask."

"The sheriff just arrested Jeremy Wright for arson."

TWELVE

Kitty sniffed the cinnamon scent appreciatively as she skirted the crystal vase on the hall table, and all but tiptoed through the elegant living room toward the kitchen. The childhood trepidation of damaging Sarah's treasures was as familiar as the strong potpourri.

Sarah's passion for style didn't end with her clothes—it extended to her house. Pink and white florals decorated the living room, and rich wooden furniture basked in the radiance from the brass lamps. Kitty felt as out of place in her dusty jeans and yellow T-shirt as Daniel appeared in his overalls and plaid shirts.

In the spacious kitchen, Daniel resided at the square pine table with a huge bowl of popcorn and plate of apple slices. She straddled a chair and plucked a handful of popcorn. "So, what do you think will happen to Jeremy?"

"Don't know what to think yet," Daniel answered grimly. "They found a flashlight near your cabin. Had his fingerprints on it."

"So? He worked the fire. Dad complained about how much equipment the firefighters lost."

"They found kerosene residue on it. Maybe from the same batch that started the Wildcat fire."

"I don't believe it."

He gazed at her, his hound dog eyes sad. "Kitty, I know you like Jeremy, but people change. There's more. Rumor has it, he confessed."

She blinked. "Confessed? To what?"

"Apparently enough for them to keep him in custody."

Why hadn't Luke said anything about Jeremy's confession to her? They were supposed to be working together. Suddenly she wasn't hungry. She passed the popcorn bowl closer to Daniel and spied a stack of large, vinyl-bound books on one of the chairs. Her heart skipped a beat. "Are those what I think they are?"

Daniel glanced down. "If you're referring to your father's scrapbooks, then yep. Thought I'd put them out in the fire department's booth."

"I searched all over the station for those."

"I'm sorry, you should've told me. I forgot they were in the house. I'd picked them up after the funeral, wanting to reminisce about the good old days." He lifted the stack and slid the books across the table to her. "Sarah insisted she wanted to go through them before we set them out, but she's so busy cooking over at the café, I'm betting she forgot. Some of the pages should be pasted down better."

"I can do it," Kitty said, flipping through pages of history that revealed stories of camaraderie, fun, bravery—and occasional tragedy. She pulled out a stapled stack of paper. "What's this?"

Daniel leaned close to study it. "I think it's minutes from the town meeting about the ski resort. Doesn't mean much now since the company bidding on the property stopped construction after the hotel burned. Don't know if, or when, they'll start up again."

"Mind if I hang on to the scrapbooks tonight?"

"Do whatever you wish. They belong to you now." He stood, stretching his arms over his head. "It's getting late. Sarah will keep both of us hopping tomorrow, getting everything ready for the festival. I imagine we'll be there all day. You don't think you...er...will be needing to go anywhere?"

Kitty studied the man who'd suddenly taken a great interest in hunting down every stray popcorn kernel on the floor. "Luke asked you to keep an eye on me, didn't he?"

He gave her a sheepish smile. "He's the boss, but I would've anyway. We never had kids, and with your pa gone, I'd like you to consider me your surrogate father."

"I can't tell you how much that means to me. Thank you." Kitty's eyes stung. "Whenever I see you, I remember the good times we had."

"I wish there'd been more." Daniel wagged a finger at her. "And I wish you'd told me what was going on."

"I'm sorry. Everything happened so quickly."

"Now that Jeremy's in jail, I reckon there shouldn't be any more danger. But I'll feel better if you're a good girl and not take any chances before you go home."

"I'll try to behave." Kitty gave Daniel a heartfelt hug and retired to the guest room. If the sheriff had his arson suspect, then why did Luke ask Daniel to watch over her? She flopped on her back in the four-poster bed and stared at the floral canopy.

Jeremy's freckled face intruded into her consciousness. Had her dad suspected Jeremy, so Jeremy killed him? Impossible. Her gut instinct refused to concede Jeremy's guilt. But maybe she was wrong, as her father might've been.

After she'd left Evan's house, she and Luke had driven to the sheriff's station, but they'd already moved Jeremy to a holding cell in Butler. Luke followed her back to Sarah's and departed without an argument over her change of address. The hollow place inside of her grew. She missed him. She missed Michael and Pastor James. What were they doing now? She'd never felt so lonely.

Unable to relax, Kitty retrieved her father's scrapbooks from the kitchen table and a glue bottle from a drawer. Sitting cross-legged on the bed, she skimmed through pages, pasting down the loose items until she came to the last book. The gray, battered cover wasn't familiar. She flipped it open and smiled at a portrait of Nana. The faded black-and-white photo revealed a young face spattered with freckles and a mischievous glint in her eyes. On the page, Sam had also pasted a school picture of Kitty and written, "The Legacy Continues." For the first time, she noticed her strong resemblance to her grandmother. Touched by her father's insight, she turned the page.

Here, her father had simply jotted "Family," and ancient pictures of strangers covered the sheet. Maybe Nana would know these relatives. One of the larger photos had popped up on one end. She lifted the glue bottle to tack it down, and realized the bumpy surface was caused by something underneath. Her fingers pulled out a deeply creased document.

The print, barely legible, appeared to be a legal document concerning property on the mountain, probably the site of her great-great-uncle's gold mine that had caved in more than fifty years ago. Her father tried several times to locate the main shaft but surmised the entrance was still buried beneath boulders. The gold vein in the mine had petered out, and the property was steep, rocky and surrounded by federal land, but for historic reasons it would still be fun to find. She tucked the document behind the photo for safe keeping.

She thumbed through the rest of the book and gasped at the mementos of her life. She found school pictures, report cards, camping photos and a program from when she'd graduated from college. A sob escaped her throat. Her seemingly indifferent father had treasured all these things, even though he'd barely acknowledged her accomplishments. He must've cared after all but just couldn't show it. He'd loved her in his own way.

Tears flowed. The painful lump of resentment she'd carried with her since her mother abandoned her on her father's doorstep melted into a sad memory.

Oh, Lord, I know it's too late to ask my dad's forgiveness, but will You please forgive me? Dad tried to do a good job. I should've tried harder to get to know him and love him while I had the chance. Help me to forget the past, to give more, and do right by the people in my life. And last, help me to forgive myself and show me what to do with my life.

"Honey, could you do me a favor?" Sarah raised her voice over the Fall Festivals blaring country music. "They're out of quarters in the bake sale booth. Could you please run over to the café and get a couple rolls?" She ran a cloth over spilled lemonade on the checkered tablecloth. "Get Clarence to open the cash register."

"Sure." Kitty said, tugging at the costume bodice that hugged her like a second skin. She lifted the long blue skirt and took a quick glance around the grassy square. Evan two-stepped with a pretty brunette in front of the bandstand, but she hadn't seen Luke since the previous evening. Her heart ached and she felt strangely incomplete without him, but it was for the best.

She swished away from the happy throng and down Main Street to the café. Faint smoke still hung in the air, but the fire burning east of town was mostly contained.

In the café, she smiled at Clarence who was swiping a mop over the floor. "Sarah sent me for some rolls of quarters."

"I just emptied the cash into the office safe, but the door isn't locked. I wanted to count it again in a few minutes."

"I thought Sarah didn't trust anyone to touch the money but herself."

"Yeah, but I have to when she's really busy." Clarence grimaced. "I hate the responsibility. She'd sack me if we came up short."

Kitty entered the café's inner sanctum, the ever-present scent of cinnamon greeting her. It was Sarah's private retreat and immaculately decorated. Not even Daniel ventured in there too often. She skirted around the cherry wood desk to the safe.

The heavy change bag snagged the safe's top drawer as she pulled, dumping its contents on the floor. Kitty groaned and dropped to her knees,

"Everything okay in there?" Clarence called, worry in his tone.

"Yeah, I'll be out in a minute." She picked up a pile of receipts and discovered a piece of pyrite. What was it with her father and Sarah's apparent obsession with the mineral? She turned the heavy rock over in her palm and examined it more closely. The solid texture seemed different. Not flaky. It couldn't be… Or could it?

Was this real gold?

The mineral composition looked similar to the rock her dad had stashed in his desk and she'd carried around in her pocket. What had happened to it? Oh, yes, the last place she'd seen it was her Jeep which she'd left at the fire station to avoid the congested parking lot by the lake.

"Everything okay in there?" Clarence asked again.

"Fine," she choked out as she finished pushing everything, including the rock, back into the safe.

"You're taking all of it?" Clarence asked.

"What?" Kitty glanced at the bag in her hand. "Yes, Sarah can count out what she needs." She hurried back to the festival, gulping deep breaths of the cool air, which caused the dress to pinch her sides. Sarah stood across the clearing by the ice cream booth. Michael held cones in both hands, one for him and one he fed to Jack. He laughed and seemed to be having a great time.

Kitty handed the change bag to one of Sarah's volunteers as her gaze skipped across the dancing crowd. Luke strode toward her, dressed in black from his cowboy hat down to his shiny boots.

He looked so dangerously attractive, Kitty couldn't speak for a moment. She snorted instead. "Who are you supposed to be? The Lone Ranger?"

"I hope not. I'm tired of being 'lone. Besides, the Lone Ranger wore a white hat." He held out his hand. "Want to take a walk?" he asked with a smile that shot tingles through her.

Kitty's better judgment screamed at her to resist him, but her resolve melted as she grasped Luke's hand and allowed him to lead her to the quiet moonlit beach. A mellow breeze blew ripples across the lake's mirrored surface. Music drifted on the pine-scented air and the stars twinkled to the beat.

Luke turned toward her. His gaze roamed over her face and searched her eyes. He leaned closer, his lips inches from her. "I'm sorry," he whispered and kissed her. A sense of belonging flowed through her and kindled a gentle, glowing fire in her heart. If she never saw Luke again, she'd remember this night, this feeling of loving someone more than herself. Which was why she had to stop this before she couldn't.

She placed her palm on his shirt and eased away from him. "Why didn't you tell me Jeremy confessed? I thought we were partners."

Luke stared at her, surprise flickering across his face, and then his stoic mask fell into place. "You were busy all day with the festival."

She crossed her arms over her chest. "You ever hear of a phone?"

"Look, it wasn't my idea for you to move to Sarah's."

"I thought some distance would be best for everyone. I don't fit in with your life. I blew it with Michael...and you."

He sighed. "No you didn't. It wasn't your fault—I over-reacted. Ever since the day I got Michael back, I've lived in fear something would happen to him again."

"He hates me."

"Michael's interpretation of hate isn't the same as yours and mine and has the lifespan of a mosquito. When you're not around, you're all he talks about. Well, except for announcing to the universe he's the most deprived child in America because he's grounded from his PlayStation."

Kitty's mouth tugged into a smile, but she shook her head. "I'm a distraction. Michael needs all your attention right now. I don't want him to feel emotionally abandoned the way I did growing up. Besides, my job is in L.A., which is where I need to be, assuming that with Jeremy's confession my father is no longer a suspect."

Luke hesitated and then nodded. "Your father is no longer a suspect in the Wildcat fire."

"I'm glad. Thank you," she said, although the words seemed inadequate. Why didn't she feel overjoyed? She'd won, her father's memory safe from ridicule. Now that they had their suspect locked up, Luke didn't need her anymore and vice versa. She was going to miss him. But she couldn't be the kind of woman he needed in his life, just like she couldn't be what Jordan wanted. She shivered with regret.

"Are you cold?" He yanked off his leather jacket and swept it around her shoulders.

"My hero." Kitty grinned, burrowing in the warm fabric. "This skimpy dress was Sarah's idea, and I better get back before she sends a posse after me."

"Wait." He grabbed the jacket lapels and drew her close again. "Will you think about coming to visit soon?"

"I don't know. Dad's gone...my cabin's in ashes. What reason would I have to come back?"

"Me." His lips brushed hers. "I think I love you."

Kitty froze. "You what?"

"After all Miranda put me through, I never expected to feel this way again. I realize the timing is bad, but I just can't get you out of mind. Maybe we should see where this thing between us leads."

Her heart banged against her ribs, taking her breath away. Could this really be happening? "But...what about Michael?"

"We'll work it out somehow." He tilted his hat back and leaned his forehead on hers. "Do you trust me?"

"I want to, but—"

Another kiss silenced her until a gruff voice called from the distance, "Chief?"

"See? Bad timing," Luke murmured and stepped away as Daniel strode toward them. "We'll talk later."

"Sarah needs you at the pickle booth to judge." He glanced from Kitty to Luke with a big grin.

Luke groaned. "Duty calls. Want to come watch me pick the best pickle in Pine Lake?"

"Wouldn't miss it, but first I need to do something," she said regretfully.

Luke shot her a questioning look as Daniel glanced over his shoulder. "Uh-oh, Sarah's heading this way."

"You better run," Kitty teased and hurried with them as far as Main Street, where Sarah slipped her arm under Luke's, guiding him swiftly along.

"I'll be there in few minutes." Kitty called to Luke as she turned on the street leading to the fire station.

He loved her. She shivered, despite the heat still lingering from his kiss. Jordan had professed love for her too, and then when the going got tough, discarded her without a backward glance. Did she dare hope Luke would be different? And what guarantee did she have that she wouldn't turn out like her mother, restless after a few years and longing to escape? Or, in turn, be like her father who'd closed himself off to the ones who loved him?

Maybe this was what Pastor James meant by having faith. Sometimes you just had to believe it was possible and make the leap.

The station bay doors stood open in honor of the festival. Light spilled out to the road, and shadows danced from moths circling the overhead lamps. She waved to George Murphy, who polished the chrome on the engine. Children crowded around the fireman, asking questions.

She ducked into her Jeep and found her father's pyrite. She held it up under the street light. Could that be real gold mixed in there?

"If you want to see if it's real, hit it with a hammer."

Kitty turned to see a short man standing by the bumper. His coat collar framed his neck and his hat brim hung low over his eyes, but she recognized the voice. "Lucky? What are you doing here? People are searching for you."

"They'd find me if I wanted to be found. Brought you something." He pulled a manila envelope from under his coat and shoved it into her hands. Kitty opened the flap and pulled out a couple of newspaper clippings and the missing pages from her father's log.

She looked at him. "You had these all along?"

Lucky's long white beard bobbed. "Sam told me to keep them hidden. I figure, as his daughter, you have a right to 'em."

"Lucky?" she asked as he turned away. "Why did my dad give you that nickname?"

He hesitated. "Because even though my son died, Sam

said I was lucky to have someone to love so much, even for a short while, just as he was lucky to have you."

"Thank you, Lucky." Kitty fought back tears as he slipped into the shadows. She spread the contents of the envelope on her car seat. The clippings were of the canyon fire, gleaned from California newspapers. Each of the articles showed photographs of the fires that'd ravished the wilderness around Pine Lake. They were dated from more than a year ago until a month before the Wildcat fire.

She set those aside and scanned the missing pages from the log book, struggling to decipher Sam's shorthand. There were several references to the new resort with phone numbers scribbled beside them. Maybe she should try calling them tomorrow.

Kitty came to the last ripped page, dated three days before Sam's death. She sat up in surprise. Her father had scribbled "Stone" on the last page and circled it. Why had her father been concerned about stones? She glanced back at the newspaper clipping of a wildlands fire that occurred a couple weeks before the Wildcat Ravine inferno, the photograph leaping out at her.

She studied the byline and fine print. The photojournalist's name wasn't mentioned. These weren't ordinary news photographs. Someone had gone to great lengths to capture the beauty and savagery of the climbing fire. Someone gifted and daring enough to take risks in the back country. Someone like—

Evan's photo of the deer fleeing a wall of fire came to mind. Did her father's note mean *Evan* Stone? She frowned. Evan said he'd been gone during the fires. What could her dad possibly want with him? Unless...

The ache in her gut confirmed what her mind didn't want to believe. She needed to see that photograph again and talk to Luke about her suspicion. Rushing as fast as her cumbersome skirt allowed, she returned to the festival and scanned the area. Luke and Michael were not among the crowd. The pickle booth was deserted.

She'd left her cell phone in her Jeep, but she still wore Luke's coat. She patted the pockets and pulled out his phone. Maybe they were with James. She flipped open the phone and searched the address book screen. She pushed a button and then realized she'd accessed Luke's messages by mistake.

Kitty started to pull the phone away from her ear when a man's voice said, "Hey, friend, I've finished tracing the daughter's financial records. Nothing. If she has overseas accounts, she hid them well. I'll be at the office until four. Oh, and that position I told you about is still open. Desk job, but steady. Get out of those sticks and consider coming back. We need you."

Who were "we"? Kitty's hit the Return Call button and got a recording.

Federal Bureau of Investigation?

The duplicity stunned her, leaving an overwhelming feeling of betrayal. Luke wanted her to trust him when he hadn't bothered to inform he'd been in the FBI? Not to mention invading her privacy and investigating her personal records? Why hadn't he trusted her enough to just ask for them? He'd duped her. Was there no one she could count on?

She thought back to her prayer the night before. She'd asked God to show her what to do with her life. Well, she just got her answer. Home to L.A. to forget the past and build a better future. One with people she could trust and who loved her without any hidden motives or agenda.

She headed back to Sarah's house and quickly changed into jeans, covering her L.A. fire department shirt with a sweatshirt. Breathless, she sat on the bed and her fingers shook as she yanked on her boots. Across the room, the vanity mirror caught her reflection of flushed cheeks and wild hair.

She'd been naive to believe things could be different. When she finished here, she'd leave Pine Lake forever.

The trembling subsided by the time she pulled up in front of the lakefront house. She pressed on the brakes. The response was sluggish. She pushed the pedal almost to the floor before the vehicle stopped. Terrific, the last thing she needed tonight was car trouble. She parked the Jeep down the street from Evan's house and strode back.

Kitty knocked. No answer. She tried the doorknob. Locked. She skirted around the side to the deck. She wedged a key along the side of the sliding glass door, and the latch popped up. Evan really needed to get a better lock. Kitty ignored the uneasy thought that she was breaking and entering. Evan wouldn't have any scruples if the situation was reversed. She just wanted to prove her suspicions were wrong so she could go home.

Using the flashlight she'd pulled out of her glove compartment, she retrieved the photograph from under the table. She recognized the mountain range in the background as the same photo in the Sacramento newspaper. If Evan had claimed to be away, then how could he have taken this shot?

The chandelier burst with light and she instinctively dived under the table.

"Come on out, Kitcat."

She slowly scooted backward and got to her feet. "Evan, I didn't know you were home."

"Obviously," he said, pointing a pistol at her head.

THIRTEEN

"I'll take that." Evan plucked the photo out of her hand and ripped it into confetti.

"Why did you leave something so incriminating lying around?" Kitty asked, forcing her gaze away from the gun. Evan's eyes glittered like cold, blue stones. Her heart thudded wildly, and she fought to stay calm.

He shrugged. "Ego has always been my downfall. This is one of my best shots ever. I nearly got toasted in the process. I'd submitted to it to the *L.A. Times,* but one of the smaller papers in Sacramento reprinted the photo. I didn't think it would matter until your dad started connecting the dots. Tragic, really."

Icy fear poured over her, shaking her to the core. "Y-You know, it would've been smarter if you'd just admitted you were in the area and shot the photograph." She slid her foot behind her and eased closer to the door. "It would've been hard to prove you were already up there before the fire started."

"Another miscalculation on my part. You were always the brains behind our little adventures." He waved the gun at her. "Where are you going? Sit down."

Kitty perched on the chair by the table. "What are you going to do? Shoot me? We're friends."

"Are we?" Evan asked with a sarcastic laugh.

She glanced at the photos on the table. One of her father, in full firefighting gear, lay on top. A sob rose in her throat. "Why, Evan?"

He looked at the picture with an incredulous expression. "I didn't kill Sam. How could you even think that?"

"You're pointing a gun at me!"

"Oh. Sorry." He lowered the weapon and grinned, some of his impishness returning. "That's only because I don't want you running off with some noble idea of turning me in before I talk sense into you. As for Sam, I liked the old grouch. He treated me better than my own worthless father."

"So why…?"

"I needed money. What else makes the world go 'round?"

"But…you make a decent living, don't you?"

"Not nearly enough." Evan sat across from her and lay the gun on the table. The muzzle faced her, and she stared at the deadly black hole. "I got in trouble. Hedged my bets wrong, and I owe lots to some really bad people. Wildlife photographers and owners of small papers don't make much. And I can't go back out in the field anymore. I saw things so horrible, you couldn't even begin to imagine." He scrubbed a hand over his face and winced when his fingers brushed the stitches on his brow. "Do you know how many nights I went to sleep thinking I wouldn't see dawn? I've lost my nerve."

His shoulders slumped. "Arson pays well, and I'm good at it. I was desperate. These people will kill me if I don't pay up. I didn't mean to hurt anyone."

He didn't *mean* to? Kitty's mind flicked over the images of Franklin lying in the hospital his life still precarious, and of her father sprawled in the ravine. And what about the people who perished in the hotel? She forced the fury from her voice and said calmly, "Evan, if you turn yourself in, they'll go easier on you. Maybe you'll get off with manslaughter."

"I told you—I didn't kill your father. I didn't set the Wildcat fire. I was supposed to, but—"

A knock on the door caused them both to jump. Evan snatched up the gun. "Move."

"Evan—"

"Please don't push me, Kitcat," he said as the knock came again. "I may not be able to bring myself to shoot you, but your friend Tanner could have a deadly accident. Even if they do get me first, someone else will finish the job." He grabbed her arm and shoved her into the foyer closet. She bumped her head on the coat railing, stifling a yelp. Her fingers found the cold knob. Locked.

The front door creaked open. "Pastor James? What can I do for you?" Evan asked, his tone radiating friendliness and concern. She'd forgotten what a good actor her friend could be.

"Hello, Mr. Stone. I was wondering if you've seen my grandson, Michael. He was at the festival earlier this evening and then disappeared. The dog, too. The sheriff and his father are out looking for him. I'm checking the houses along the lake."

"I haven't seen him lately, but I'll keep an eye out for him."

"Appreciate it." The door clicked shut and Evan uttered a curse. "Stupid woman. She's going to ruin everything."

Kitty beat on the door with her fists. "Evan! What's going on? Do you know what happened to Michael?"

"Shut up and stay put. Remember what I said about Tanner. I'll settle things with you when I get back." The floor vibrated as he strode away and then the front door slammed.

Grabbing the garment pole over her head, Kitty braced against the back wall and kicked on the door paneling with all her strength. The wood bowed and she tried again, this time striking with her boot heels. The wood gave way. Slivers scratched deep lines in her wrist as she wiggled her fingers through the hole and turned the lock.

Evan's truck peeled out of the driveway as she ran to the phone. Dead. No time to look for another. She'd left Luke's phone at Sarah's, but hers was still in the Jeep.

She dashed outside. No lights shone from the cabin windows lining the street. Everyone must still be at the festival. In the distance, Evan's headlights turned on one of the many dirt roads snaking through the forest behind town. She didn't dare lose sight of him. Instinctively, she knew he'd lead her to Michael. She jumped in her Jeep and tore down the street to the entrance of the service road Evan must've taken. She slammed on the brakes and the pedal sank to the floor before the tires grabbed the gravel and she skidded around the turn.

She pumped the pedal again, with even less response. Must be leaking brake fluid. Her heart hammered. She'd only have a few more attempts before they failed completely.

She fumbled in her bag for her cell phone. She held it up, the tiny screen glowing. No bars on this side of the valley where the hill blocked the tower. She threw the phone on the seat and concentrated on not plunging over the cliff.

Gravity slowed the Jeep as she crossed high above the town before the rough road thrust her downward again. Trees crowded on both sides as she shot through the forest. Another hairpin turn loomed. She shouldered the tires next to the embankment. At the last second before being hurled into space, she punched the brakes and yanked hard on the wheel. The passenger door screeched as it sideswiped the bank. The Jeep hurdled around the corner. Suddenly, Evan's truck appeared in her headlights and she slammed into his bumper, knocking both vehicles off the narrow road.

Kitty clawed the airbag away from her face and shoved the gear in Reverse. Tires spun. The Jeep rocked. Shaking, she climbed out to find the axle hung on a boulder. Now what? Evan's truck listed too far on the hill to be of any use. But no matter, he had to be around here somewhere.

She scrambled up the embankment. The Jeep headlights shone out into space. Maybe someone would spot the beams and come to help. Wishing for her flashlight, she waited for her eyes to adjust to the shadows. Above her rose a dry rock bed, left by an ancient glacier. On either side were dense woods, piled thick with pine needles.

Voices drifted toward her only to be blown about in the wind, making it difficult to pinpoint their location. Kitty ran forward, arms outstretched as branches whipped at her face. One of the voices grew louder, angry and more distinct. Evan!

"Let him go. He's unconscious and won't remember a thing when he wakes up. We don't need more blood on our hands."

Kitty dropped to the ground. Pine needles and twigs dug into her knees as she crawled closer.

"I've come too far to give it all up now," a husky female voice said. "It'll just be another tragic accident caused by the crazed arsonist. Only this time, they'll catch him."

"You can't do that! They'll know it wasn't Jeremy, even if he was stupid enough to confess to a crime he didn't commit." Kitty scooted on her belly and peered into the clearing. Evan stood in front of her, blocking her view.

"So? He had an accomplice."

"You're insane. I'll—" A deafening shot rang out.

Evan screamed and crumbled to the ground. Kitty shrank deeper into the brush. She peered past his prone form. Michael lay motionless on the ground. Luke sat beside him, blood trickling down his forehead. He hunched over, one hand clutching his shoulder and the other on Michael.

"I'm sorry, but you shouldn't have tried to blackmail me, Evan. You selfish pig. You should've been satisfied with what you got." Shock riveted through her as Kitty finally recognized the hoarse voice. Sarah emerged from the shadows and poked a gun against Luke's neck. "Come on, we have work to do."

Luke slowly got to his feet and swayed, fighting to remain upright. "Forget it, Sarah. You'll have to finish this on your own."

Sarah pointed the gun at Michael. "I'll kill him now."

"No!"

"Then come, and don't try to run. I can shoot the ear off a squirrel at a hundred yards."

They disappeared into the woods, and Kitty burst out of the shadows, landing on Evan's chest. He groaned. "Quiet," she whispered. "At least you're not dead. Where'd she get you?"

"My thigh. She wants to make me suffer." Evan groaned again and lifted a bloody hand. "Sarah's lost her mind. She's going to set the forest on fire to cover her tracks."

Kitty reached under Evan and extracted his gun. She checked to make sure the safety was on and shoved it under her belt. "Where'd they go?"

"Over to an abandoned mine where I stored kerosene." Evan propped himself on his elbows and gazed at the widening red stain on his pants. "I'm going to bleed to death."

"Put my sweatshirt over the wound and wrap your belt around as tight as you can." She tossed her sweatshirt to Evan and leaned over Michael. "What did she do to him?"

"Drugged. Got the dog too."

The ice cream at the festival, Kitty surmised as Evan continued, "She wanted Tanner to follow her here, so she took the kid. Threatened to harm Michael if Tanner didn't cooperate." Evan moaned. "She panicked when I told her Luke was a FBI agent."

"How did you find out?"

"With Franklin's wonderful search engine before it blew up. I found some buried news stories about a Chicago kidnapping. Then this morning I finally was able to contact a close family friend of Pastor James in Chicago. I tricked him into spilling enough details for me to connect the dots. Am I good or what?" He closed his eyes. "I didn't think Sarah would go this far...."

"We have to get out of here." Kitty pulled Michael up by the arms and draped him over her back and shoulders. The cold gun dug into her belly. "Stand up, Evan, or you're going to die here."

He shook his head, eyes still closed. "Just take the boy and run before it's too late."

"Quit being such a baby. The Evan I knew would fight."

"My photographs will be worth more after I'm gone," he murmured.

Kitty gasped with exasperation and nudged him hard with her boot. "Evan Stone, if you don't get up right now, I'll shred every one of your photos myself. No one will ever see them."

His eyes snapped open. "Has anyone ever mentioned you have a mean streak?" He grabbed the trunk of a skinny pine and staggered up.

"Hang on to me if you need to." Determination, chased by fear, surged through her as she lunged forward, propelling them toward the service road.

"Now tell me what's going on," she asked, panting. "If I die, at least I want to know why."

"Gold," Evan said as he stumbled from one tree to the

next. "There's an old gold mine above one of the new ski runs. Belonged to a great-uncle of Sam's."

"I know about the mine. The gold petered out."

"Those earthquakes a few years back must've unearthed another small vein. Sam must've told Sarah because she funded the purchase of mining equipment. They secretly extracted gold until the resort construction began."

"How did you get involved?"

"By accident. I was photographing in the area. They had to cut me in or—"

"You'd expose them. I get it. Greed." She stopped to catch her breath. "Sarah hired you to start fires to frighten off potential investors who might discover the mine."

"Yeah, she wasn't sure what the legalities were for extracting gold from government land, even if your family had an old claim. And then there's the tax consequences. She convinced your father they'd worry about all that after they got the gold. Everything was going according to plan until the company who bought the ski resort refused to be scared away."

Kitty glanced behind them. Panicky fear for Luke constricted her chest. She pulled Michael higher on her shoulders and plunged ahead. She had to keep moving, keep talking, or her heart would shatter into a million pieces. "What happened to my father?"

Evan's face loomed ghostly pale in the moonlight. "Sam was furious when he discovered I'd been setting the fires. He told Sarah to knock it off or he'd shut her down. Also he found religion, and I think he wanted to come clean. So, somehow she lured him up to Wildcat Ravine. I suspect she pushed him over the edge. I arrived...too late. She started the fire and it was her idea to frame Sam." He struggled to catch his breath. "She found one of his papers from the Bible Study and made it look like he was still involved with SOLO. She's good at copying handwriting, but it was a stupid idea.

With analysis they would've known it wasn't Sam's. Then I couldn't find it at your dad's cabin and—"

"How did you know it was in my bag?"

"Lucky find. I got in through Tanner's attic window and snooped around to see what you'd uncovered." He whimpered. "This whole thing is your fault anyway. If you hadn't come back to Pine Lake, I would've had time to find your father's gold nuggets—and whatever other incriminating stuff he'd left behind—without having to burn down the cabin... or play these stupid cat-and-mouse games."

"G-games?" Kitty sputtered, outraged. "You could've killed me with that shovel or burned me to death."

"Oh, give me a break. I only grazed you with the shovel, and I missed you with the pinecone on purpose. And I knew you weren't in your dad's cabin when I lit it. I was just trying to scare you into going home. You can't take a hint."

"What about shooting at me in the canyon? That wasn't a hint. That was war!"

"Hey, don't pin that on me. Sarah had no patience and took the sniper rifle I'd gotten from an old army buddy. She would've hit you if she wanted to."

"That's supposed to be comforting?" Kitty said, consumed with hurt and fury. "So...who called me in L.A. to come home?"

"Probably Jeremy. He kept nosing around trying to prove your father's innocence, the stupid kid."

No wonder Jeremy hadn't seemed surprised to see her. "But why would he confess to something he didn't do?"

"Who knows? He's a nut, but a loyal one." Evan groaned and collapsed against a tree trunk. "I can't go any farther."

"You have to." Kitty bumped him forward. "Keep talking. Why did you start setting fires again? You'd already framed my dad."

"The cash stopped flowing, and I needed to remind Sarah how easily I could expose it all."

"You're insane."

"At times," he said as they slid down the last embankment to the deserted road. "Hey, you smashed my new truck!"

"Serves you right for cutting my brake lines." She glared at him. "Besides, how can you get upset about a fender bender after blowing up a building?"

He wagged a finger at her. "Don't pin that one on me, either. I think Sarah rigged that explosion to get Franklin and she didn't care if I went, too. He was asking too many questions. But she didn't count on him being such a tough old bird. He's going make it."

"Let's hope *we* survive, too. Come on, we need to find Luke's truck," she said as a terrible roaring sound swelled below. Flames shot up the mountainside toward them, the wind causing the flames to leap from tree to tree. Sarah must have ignited the kerosene.

"We can't outrun it," Evan shouted.

Kitty looked frantically around them. He was right…no escape. They were going to burn to death.

Okay God, if ever I needed You, it's right now. Please help me get Michael out of this. I've made a mess of my life, but he deserves a chance to live.

"Fire shelters!" screamed through her brain. Her fire shelters were still in the Jeep. *Thank You, God.*

Her eyes focused on the large ravine to the east with few trees and lots of giant boulders. "Evan, take Michael and head for the rocks. Stay away from the trees and brush."

"I can't." Evan moaned. "I'm done for."

"Yes, you can! You owe me that much." Kitty lowered Michael beside him. "Drag Michael up there. I'll be right back." She sprinted for her Jeep, pulling out the two yellow packs. A dark cloud of smoke engulfed her. She yanked her collar over her mouth. Fire crackled in the distance, and then a gunshot rang out.

Luke! She froze, fighting the urge to race toward the sound. She glanced at Michael in Evan's arms. She knew what Luke would want her to do. Save his son. Grabbing Michael from Evan, she charged up the hill.

"Run and don't look back," Kitty cried, slipping on the loose gravel. Her breaths came in short gasps. A scorching wind lashed her back. Flames flew overhead, igniting trees on both sides of the ravine. Evan tripped and fell. She set Michael down, opened a pack and shook the fire shelter free.

"Evan, grab this and hold it over you." She tucked one end under his feet and pulled the shelter over his head.

Kitty seized Michael and moved farther into the safety of ravine. Heat licked her face. The smell of singed hair filled her nostrils. Gasping, she lay Michael on the ground and yanked out the other fire shelter. She stepped on one end, pulled the fabric over her shoulders and fell forward across Michael. Her elbows hit the ground first, shooting jarring pain up her shoulders and down her back. She held tight to the fabric as a roar like a freight train howled over them.

Michael moaned, his mouth near her ear. "Lie still," she said, squeezing him tighter with her elbows. "It'll be over soon." One way or another.

Michael wiggled again and Kitty pressed harder against him. "We're in a fire shelter, Michael. If we get out, we'll get burned."

"Fire shelter? Oh, cool." He stopped squirming. "Where's my dad? Did Miss Sarah hurt him?"

Kitty bit her lip, trying not to imagine Luke dead from a gunshot wound. "The last time I saw him, he was walking."

A deafening crash reverberated through the air. The earth vibrated beneath them with the impact. They both jerked.

"Trees," Kitty said, hoping they'd gotten far enough into the ravine.

"Miss Kitty, am I going to die?"

She hugged him tighter. "I won't let you."

"I don't want to leave my dad again. I never told him, but it was my fault I got kidnapped last time. I didn't wait where I was supposed to. This man wanted me to help look for his puppy and—"

"Listen to me. What happened to you wasn't your fault," she said over the hard knot in her throat. "Just like it wasn't my fault for what happened with my parents. Sometimes bad things happen, but we just need faith that God will help us through the bad stuff and we'll become better, stronger people."

Michael sniffed and didn't reply as peace washed over Kitty. The roaring lessened, and she dared to lift the flap of the shelter. The wind had blown the fire over them, and in its wake, the blackened trees still smoldered. Thick smoke obscured the ravine. Her eyes watered. "Just a few more minutes, and we'll go."

"Know what?" Michael said. "I prayed someone would find us. You're an answer to a prayer."

Tears welled. "Oh Michael, no one has ever said that to me before." she said, her words nearly drowned out by a loud cracking sound. Something heavy fell on her shoulder, pinning her against Michael. Pain shot through her, and heat seared the fabric. "Michael! I can't move. Get out and head to the top of mountain. They'll find you there."

She clenched her jaw as he shook his head in protest. "You can get help!"

Michael whimpered, but he wiggled out from under her. Suddenly, the weight lifted and the shelter was ripped back.

Luke stood over them, hefting a huge branch of a burning sapling further away from them.

"Dad!" Michael shouted.

Sparks bounced off Luke's hair as he drew Michael close. "Are you hurt?"

Michael shook his head, and Luke squatted close to Kitty. "Can you move?"

Kitty gasped. "You're alive."

Luke leaned his ash-covered face close to hers. "Kitty, focus. Can you move?"

"I think so." Ignoring the rush of pain, she flung her arms around his neck, her lips meeting his. He froze for a second and then kissed her back.

"Um...Dad?" Michael asked with a giggle.

Luke lifted his head, but she tightened her hold, pressing her cheek against his. "I love you, Luke Tanner." Kitty whispered in to his ear, relieved and grateful she'd been given the chance to tell him.

"It's a miracle," Luke said hoarsely, his hand grabbing Michael's. "I can't believe I found you."

"God saved us," Kitty said. Copious tears spilled over and cooled her face. She'd never cried as much as she had in the past couple of weeks. Her reputation as a tough broad would be shot if she didn't control herself. She swiped the tears away as she assessed the damage created by Sarah's bullet. Dried blood stained Luke's torn sleeve. "Are you okay?"

Luke glanced at his shoulder. "Just a flesh wound. We better move. If the wind shifts, we'll be trapped."

"Evan's down there." She pointed to the other fire shelter, stark yellow against the rocks. He'd been far enough away; the burning tree missed him.

Relief spread across his face. "Is he still alive?"

"I think so," she said. "But he's weak. I don't know if he can climb to the top. What he did was horrendous, but he did try to help Michael. We can't just leave him, even if he's depraved. What if another tree falls?"

"I can help you, Dad," Michael said, gazing up at him. "We can do this."

Luke smoothed the hair from his son's forehead. "You're right. *We* can."

She followed Luke down, yanked back the fire shelter, and lifted Evan to his feet. He mumbled something incomprehensible and then sagged. Luke caught him under the arms and hauled him up the ravine. Kitty grabbed the fire shelters and followed, sticking close to Michael. They took turns lifting Evan's feet as they scaled higher over the giant boulders and around fallen pines.

Her ribs ached and her body dripped with sweat by the time they reached the mountain summit. A bruise darkened her arm where the tree had smashed into her, but, so far, adrenaline kept most of the pain at bay.

She collapsed on the smooth, cool rock. Dawn broke over the horizon, and she gazed around them. They were protected on the massive granite plateau, but the fire below cut off any routes to safety.

"What now?" Kitty forced the words out of her parched throat.

Luke's drenched T-shirt heaved from the exertion of the rapid climb. "A forestry service plane or helicopter should easily spot us."

"A helicopter?" Michael's dirty face broke into a big grin. "Awesome! Wait until Austin hears I got to ride in a helicopter." He scampered with renewed energy to an outcropping where he could scan the sky.

Luke eased Evan to the ground next to her. Evan's eyes rolled back, and he slumped over. Kitty placed two fingers on his neck and checked his pulse, which wasn't as strong as she'd like. His skin felt cool and clammy.

Shock.

She elevated his feet on a rock and wrapped the fire shelter sheet around him. "Evan, just hang in there, okay? I'm praying for you."

Luke sat next to her as they watched the firestorm blast its way through the forest. She told him what Evan had revealed about Sarah and the gold mine.

"Well, that explains where your father got money to pay for your grandmother's fancy retirement accommodations," he said. "If your family had legal claim on the mine, the gold should be yours. Might take some time and red tape, though. Can you prove ownership?"

"The deed is in one of his scrapbooks. I found it last night." A thrill of relief shot through her. "Actually, if there is any gold left, it'll go to Nana."

"There's the sticky subject of taxes your father didn't pay."

She nodded. "I'll take care of it. I believe he was going to do the right thing but didn't get the chance. I can live with that. He had his faults, but he was a good man, and he loved me."

"Then that's all that matters. We'll fix it with the IRS," Luke said. "But Evan will face charges of arson and probably accessory to murder since he was with Sarah when she set the Wildcat fire."

Kitty checked Evan's weak pulse again, sorrow welling for the man who'd once been her friend. But he'd brought this on himself and would have to face the consequences. She looked at Luke and mouthed, "Sarah?"

He lowered his voice so Michael couldn't hear. "If she'd gotten in her car instead of trying to kill me, she would've made it out in time. There's a high probability she didn't." He slid his arm around her shoulders, offering comfort.

Kitty's gaze shifted to the clearing and the road where

they'd been. Flames consumed the entire area. What a waste. Sorrow laced with fury welled. Eventually she'd come to terms about the woman who'd been so much a part of her childhood. Greed had almost destroyed everyone she loved. Right now, she'd concentrate on her second chance on life.

Thank You, God, for saving them. And me...

She wiped her eyes and leaned against Luke. Pine Lake winked at them in the distance. The fire had moved east away from town.

Luke tilted his cheek to rest on her head. "I'll be eternally grateful to you, Kitty, for getting Michael out of there. I'd been looking for him in town when Sarah drove up. She had a gun on him and threatened to kill him if I didn't go with her. After we reached the clearing and she shot Evan, she needed me to roll back the boulders in front of the mine where Evan stored kerosene. She had me carry the canisters back up the hill. When she leveled the gun at me again, I managed to throw fuel in her face and run."

Kitty shivered. "I arrived when she shot Evan. I didn't know what to do."

"You did great, although I was frantic when I couldn't find Michael in the clearing. I figured Stone took him and prayed they'd made it out ahead of the fire. I barely got to the ravine in time to find a hole under a boulder when the fire swept by." He let out a sharp, angry breath. "We should've nabbed Sarah sooner when we'd discovered she'd been funneling money into overseas holdings. It seemed too much to be coming from her diner."

"How could you know for sure though? Jeremy confessed."

"Yeah, that's another thing I need to clear up," he replied. "Jeremy confessed all right, but only to lighting matches as a kid and starting a small brush fire. The sheriff arrested him, but it became obvious the evidence against him was planted. It was Jeremy's idea for us to hold him in custody to let the real arsonist think he was successful in framing him, and maybe let down his guard. We just let everyone assume Jeremy was guilty."

Kitty bristled. "Including me."

Luke placed a finger under her chin, turning her to face him. "I wanted you out of danger."

She sighed and used her thumb to brush away gray ash clinging to his cheek. "As long as you don't conceal anything from me ever again."

He cleared his throat. "There's something else I need to tell you, Kitty."

"That you're in the FBI?"

His eyebrows lifted. "*Ex*-FBI. I quit after I got Michael back but agreed to temporarily work with them again when we thought SOLO might be involved in the fires. How did you find out?"

"I mistakenly accessed your phone messages and heard a message about tracing my financial records."

His eyes flickered with regret. "It was routine. I ordered the trace before you got here. I should've told you."

"Yes, you should've, but it doesn't matter now." Nothing mattered except they were safe and together again.

"Copter!" Michael yelled as the mechanical bird swooped over them. Unable to land, it hovered, making speech impossible over the beating blades. A cable dangling a litter descended from the aircraft. Kitty and Luke strapped the unconscious Evan onto it. After he was safely aboard, they sent Michael up.

"Your turn." Luke pulled Kitty into his arms and tenderly kissed her before the cable hoisted her heavenward. A ranger grabbed her and hauled her inside the helicopter. He unfastened the cable and she scrambled to a seat. A paramedic worked over Evan, sliding an IV needle into his arm. Michael watched, his eyes glowing with interest.

"Are you okay, Miss McGuire?" Sheriff Johnson asked from his position by the pilot.

She nodded and shouted back. "Am I ever glad to see you!"

"In all my born days I never thought I'd ever hear you say that," the sheriff said with a chuckle.

"Where's Jack?" Michael asked, his eyes round with fear. "Where's my dog?"

"He's at the vet and going to be fine," Johnson said, and Michael let out a whoop.

Luke strapped himself into the seat beside her and grinned. "This will make quite a story for your buddies back home. You know, I've been thinking lately that maybe Michael and I wouldn't mind living part-time in L.A."

Kitty bit her lip to keep from smiling as the helicopter dipped and headed for the Butler hospital. She shook her head. "I don't think that's a good idea."

"Okay…." The grin slipped from his face. "I can't blame you for not wanting to be reminded of what happened here, but we consider you family now…and family sticks together. We won't give you up easily."

"Is that a threat?"

"Well…sure."

Her lips tugged into a smile. "What I meant was that the city is no place to raise a kid like Michael, at least not right now. Not when he's going to be a local hero at school for outrunning a firestorm and riding in a helicopter."

Luke's eyes widened. "What are you saying?"

"I'm saying this place isn't so bad. I like feeling a part of the community and church. People made mistakes, but so did I. If I can forgive them and my family, then I can forgive myself too. With God's help, I'm ready to make a fresh start."

"Y-you'd be willing to give up your job?"

"Not exactly." Kitty grinned. "I'm making a strategic career move. I'm assuming there may be an opening in the Pine Lake Fire Department soon when the current fire chief decides to run for sheriff. Right, Johnson?"

"Couldn't think of a better man for the position," Johnson said. "I'm retiring next month and going fishing before the snow flies. Sheriff Tanner has a nice ring to it."

"Maybe." Luke glanced at his son. "I'll have to think about it."

"It's going to be so cool! I'll get to ride in the sheriff car without even being in trouble," Michael said with an impish grin that caused Luke to roll his eyes.

Kitty laughed. "Meanwhile, I'm going get my dad's property back and rebuild the cabin. I'm hoping to spend time with you all when I can. I'm not great with housework, cooking or knowing how to raise kids, but hey, if I can jump into burning buildings, I certainly can give this a shot. What do you thin—

Luke smothered her words with a kiss and then gazed into her eyes. "Kitty McGuire, I love you just the way you are." He kissed her again, and any lingering doubt evaporated into a cloud of joy as love swept Kitty from her singed head to her aching toes.

The sheriff coughed loudly, and she pulled away from Luke, glancing around the cabin. Michael was pestering the paramedic with endless questions, but Evan winked at her with a knowing smirk. Her jaw clenched. Relief that he'd regained consciousness warred with bitter resentment for what he'd put them through. Forgiving him wasn't going to be easy, but if she were ever to have peace, she had to try.

She gave him a small, reassuring nod before he closed his eyes again.

Luke leaned forward. "Hey, I'm trying to ask you something."

Her pulse quickened at the seriousness in his expression. "What is it?"

"I know I may be rushing things, but after what happened today, life seems way too short and unpredictable. So I'm just going to jump in and say this. You don't have to decide now, but Kitty, will you marry me? You know, when we get to know each other better. Someday? Soon?"

"Is that all?" Kitty laughed, sending up a prayer of thanks. "Just try and stop me." She snuggled under his arm in utter contentment as the helicopter swept by the majestic Four Sisters. She could hardly wait to land in Pine Lake.

Through the ashes of her past, Kitty's heart had come home at last.

* * * * *

Dear Reader,

I hope you enjoyed reading *Firestorm*. The inspiration for this book came from the years I served as a part-time firefighter in a small, quiet town similar to Pine Lake. Although I didn't see much action, I'll never forget the training sessions or the camaraderie. They forged a deep gratitude for our men and women in uniform who willingly put their lives on the line to save others.

Like firefighters who face the flames, sometimes our faith can be tested by the trails of life. I hope the story of Kitty and Luke reaffirmed that when times are tough, we're sheltered by God's promise that if our faith is genuine we'll receive His glory, honor and praise.

I'd love to hear from readers. You can contact me through my Web site at www.KellyAnnRiley.com.

May your faith remain forever strong,

Kelly Ann Riley

QUESTIONS FOR DISCUSSION

1. Kitty and her father parted on angry words, and she never had the chance to say she was sorry. Have you ever had regrets about a relationship or had unresolved anger toward someone? What does the Bible say about anger? (See *Ephesians* 4:31-32, *Psalm* 37:8).

2. Tragedy and heartache can tear a family apart. What helped Luke get through the ordeal of his son's kidnapping and rebuild a life in Pine Lake?

3. After Michael's kidnapping, Luke is understandably overprotective of his son. How did this affect his relationship with Michael? With Kitty? Pastor James suggested that Luke pray about it. How do you deal with fear and worry?

4. Luke, Michael and Kitty have issues with learning to trust each other. Kitty made a mistake when she assumed Michael had told Luke he'd been in the *Tribune* building. Should she have handled the situation differently? If so, how? Do you agree with Kitty that Luke should've told her he'd been a FBI agent and was using his contacts to investigate her? How do you feel about police and FBI agents working undercover? Does the end justify the means?

5. Kitty and Luke are first responders and are trained in cardiopulmonary resuscitation and first aid. Do you think

it's important that the public learn CPR and emergency first aid? Are you certified in CPR? If not, do you feel a need to get trained? Why? Or why not?

6. After Kitty visits the church and reconnects with childhood acquaintances, how does her opinion of the church change? What important roles can a church family provide to an individual? How can you make others feel welcome in your church?

7. As it says in *John* 8:32, the truth shall set you free. Once Kitty discovered the scrapbooks and realized how much her father had cared for her, she was able to forgive him and herself for the past. This opened her heart to receive love again. Should Kitty also forgive Sarah and Evan for what they did? How does one forgive terrible crimes?

8. Sarah seemed to have a good life. She had nice clothes, owned a successful business and had a beautiful home, yet she let her greed for gold cause her to do terrible things. How can we protect ourselves from crossing the line from wanting nice possessions in our lives to being greedy?

9. Kitty realized that even if her heart was shattered by circumstances, God would be there to pick up the pieces. Has there ever been a moment in your life where you faced difficult choices and just had to step out in faith? What was the outcome?

10. Kitty and Luke fell in love while working to solve her father's case. During intense circumstances such as these,

sometimes people tend to bond quickly. If you were Kitty or Luke, what additional steps might you take to ensure a strong marriage?

11. The theme scripture for *Firestorm* is 1 *Peter* 1:7 and is about faith tested by fire. What are some of your favorite Bible verses about faith?

SUSPENSE

TITLES AVAILABLE NEXT MONTH

Available August 10, 2010

ASSIGNMENT: BODYGUARD
Lenora Worth

PROTECTIVE CUSTODY
Lynette Eason

VANISHING ACT
Liz Johnson

SILENT PROTECTOR
Barbara Phinney

LISCNM0710

HARLEQUIN®

A Romance

FOR EVERY MOOD™

Spotlight on
Heart & Home

Heartwarming romances
where love can happen
right when you least expect it.

See the next page to enjoy a sneak peek
from Harlequin® American Romance®,
a Heart and Home series.

*Five hunky Texas single fathers—five stories from
Cathy Gillen Thacker's* LONE STAR DADS *miniseries.
Here's an excerpt from the latest, THE MOMMY PROPOSAL
from Harlequin American Romance.*

"I hear you work miracles," Nate Hutchinson drawled.
Brooke Mitchell had just stepped into his lavishly appointed
office in downtown Fort Worth, Texas.

"Sometimes, I do." Brooke smiled and took the sexy
financier's hand in hers, shook it briefly.

"Good." Nate looked her straight in the eye. "Because
I'm in need of a home makeover—fast. The son of an old
friend is coming to live with me."

She was still tingling from the feel of his warm palm.
"Temporarily or permanently?"

"If all goes according to plan, I'll adopt Landry by
summer's end."

Brooke had heard the founder of Nate Hutchinson
Financial Services was eligible, wealthy and generous to a
fault. She hadn't known he was in the market for a family,
but she supposed she shouldn't be surprised. But Brooke
had figured a man as successful and handsome as Nate
would want one the old-fashioned way. *Not that this was
any of her business…*

"So what's the child like?" she asked crisply, trying not
to think how the marine-blue of Nate's dress shirt deepened
the hue of his eyes.

"I don't know." Nate took a seat behind his massive
antique mahogany desk. He relaxed against the smooth
leather of the chair. "I've never met him."

"Yet you've invited this kid to live with you permanently?"

"It's complicated. But I'm sure it's going to be fine."

Obviously Nate Hutchinson knew as little about teenage

boys as he did about decorating. But that wasn't her problem. Finding a way to do the assignment without getting the least bit emotionally involved was.

Find out how a young boy brings Nate and Brooke together in THE MOMMY PROPOSAL,
coming August 2010 from Harlequin American Romance.

HARLEQUIN
Ambassadors

Want to share your passion for reading Harlequin® Books?

Become a Harlequin Ambassador!

Harlequin Ambassadors are a group of passionate and well-connected readers who are willing to share their joy of reading Harlequin® books with family and friends.

You'll be sent all the tools you need to spark great conversation, including free books!

All we ask is that you share the romance with your friends and family!

You'll also be invited to have a say in new book ideas and exchange opinions with women just like you!

To see if you qualify* to be a Harlequin Ambassador, please visit
www.HarlequinAmbassadors.com.

*Please note that not everyone who applies to be a Harlequin Ambassador will qualify. For more information please visit www.HarlequinAmbassadors.com.

Thank you for your participation.

BAP098-PA

Love Inspired
HISTORICAL

INSPIRATIONAL HISTORICAL ROMANCE

Bestselling author

JILLIAN HART

**brings readers
a new heartwarming story in**

Patchwork Bride

Meredith Worthington is returning to
Angel Falls, Montana, to follow her dream
of becoming a teacher. And perhaps get to know
Shane Connelly, the intriguing new wrangler on
her father's ranch. Shane can't resist her charm
even though she reminds him of everything he'd like
to forget. But will love have time to blossom before
she discovers the secret he's been hiding all along?

*Available in August
wherever books are sold.*

Steeple
Hill®

www.SteepleHill.com

LIH82841